# THE FOLKS

RAY GARTON

For Dawn…

# One

On the morning of a day when thoughts turn to the dead rising from their graves, I stood by while one of the dead was put into hers. Carla Firth. I had dated her once last spring, just before I dropped out of college. It had been a terrible date, but only because we had nothing in common, nothing to talk about. She was a pretty blonde, funny, and she never hesitated to look me in the eye, never turned quickly away from my face. A nice girl. Of course, she had to be to go out with me. She was a political science major and all she could talk about was the upcoming presidential election. She was a Republican and thought George W. Bush would not only win, but would be one of the best presidents the country's ever had. She and a few other students had attended the Republican convention in Philadelphia back in July. Her best friend, a chubby Korean girl named Lisa, had been on the news the night before. She'd tearfully told the reporter that the last time she saw Carla, she was still riding on the high she'd gotten from the convention. But on that rainy October morning, she was riding in a black metal box with brass handles, down into the ground. Her body torn and mangled by someone, her pretty face mutilated. Happy Halloween.

The sky was the color of rotting teeth and an indifferent drizzle pattered on all the black umbrellas around the open grave. Someone—I think it was Carla's mother—wailed, and the sound seemed to hover over the gathering even after she stopped.

It had been quiet until then. The sound went through me like steel. The withering sobs that followed were almost worse. My signal to leave. I have never been able to tolerate the sound of crying. Even if I know better, I am always certain that I'm the cause.

Everyone called it simply The Village but its real name was Pinecrest. It was halfway up Mt. Crag and overlooked the town of the same name below. The Granite River ran by at the foot of the mountain, and the bridge that crossed it and led into the town of Mount Crag sometimes flooded in the winter. When that happened, many of the college students on the hill—mostly those who were there against their will, put there by parents who thought a Christian education would do them some good—were cut off from their supply of beer, liquor, and cigarettes.

The town of Mount Crag was a greeting card. The sidewalks were always clean, lawns and hedges were always neat and green. The old Methodist church in the center of town was over a hundred years old, white with a steeple and a bell that rang at six in the morning, noon, six in the evening, and midnight. There was a Safeway on one side of town, and a locally owned market called Shop-Rite on the other. The diner was owned by Carrie Lodge, single mother of two boys, Keith and Evan, eight and ten respectively. It was called the Pantry Shelf, but everyone referred to it simply as the diner.

It had taken a while for me to muster the courage to go into the diner the first time. I was pretty sure I would not be welcome. People do not want to see me while they're eating. But Carrie made me feel welcome. I'd been eating breakfast and dinner there since Grandma stopped talking to me, and we had gotten to know each other pretty well.

I scared Carrie's boys at first, but we soon became friends, too. Most kids are initially scared of me, but their fears are much easier to allay than the ones hiding behind the smiles of the perfectly controlled adults. All I have to do with kids is tell them how it happened. I tell them about waking up in the hospital afterward, seeing my new face for the first time months later. I tell it like a story, and by the time I'm done, they're smiling and I'm a hero for surviving it all. Even the ones who cry the first time they see me are fine with it after that, once they understand it.

Adults, on the other hand, see my face and know perfectly well what happened without being told, and yet they see only themselves, because they know it could happen to them. Or to a spouse, a child, a lover. *What would I do?* they wonder, and the thought is as plain on their faces as their forced, rigid smiles.

When I first came to Pinecrest to live with Grandma, I used to get stared at a lot.

Even laughed at. But I found if I introduced myself to everyone I met, staring and laughing became harder to do because suddenly I had a name and I was a person, not just a hideous pink face made up of mangled strips of scar tissue. I had no hair on the left side of my head, so I took extra care to keep what I had left neatly trimmed and combed. Always dressed as well as I could, tried to present myself well. I had a lot to make up for.

The people of Mount Crag referred to the people of Pinecrest as "them Christian folks on the mountain." It was noncommittal, but most of them disliked the Christians and their college intensely. Even many of the Christians who lived in Mount Crag kept their distance from those on the mountain. The students of the College of the Hand of God put on various revivals and programs in town every year for extra credit. Few ever showed up. Some of the students roamed Mount Crag day after day, handing out literature and trying to convert the townspeople. It wasn't an easy job because nobody was interested.

I attended Hand of God for almost one year. Out of the blue, Grandma received a letter from the president of the college, Dr. Elijah Morton, saying that an anonymous benefactor had set up a college fund for me, and I was to begin the next semester.

Grandma was thrilled, of course, because she thought I would finally see the light and accept Jesus Christ as my personal lord and savior. I had been hearing that for so long, it did not mean anything anymore. It sounded like "New and Improved," or "Money Back Guarantee." Meant nothing.

I knew it had to be one of the Bollingers. Who else could it be? I sure didn't have any rich relatives, and if it *was* one of my relatives, then it had to be a scam. Maybe it was something the Bollingers did regularly, although I had never heard anything about it.

The family had dwindled over the decades, and what was left of the Bollingers lived on the opposite side of Mt. Crag from the town. Their odd house was a series of blocky structures that crawled up the mountain between jutting shelves of gray rock.

I had seen it only from a distance. It was enormous and looked as old as the mountain, yet it was still innovative in its bizarre combination of organic and art deco architecture. It stood out boldly from the trees and rocks, all sharp corners and graceful lines, and yet, at certain angles—and the angles never seemed to be exactly the same twice—it dissolved like a mirage to become more trees and rocks, just another part of the mountain. There were other houses up there that had been lived in, at one time or another, by some of the Bollingers, all of them huge and ominous, but long empty, rotting under twisted, smothering vines and entered only by the wild animals that made the mountain their home. Only the gigantic structure on the other side of the mountain remained occupied and maintained. It was the only one that looked alive.

No one was sure how many Bollingers lived there. A woman named Amanda Bollinger was occasionally dropped off in the middle of town by a long, old, shiny, black limousine that smacked of wartime Germany. Or *The Addams Family*. I don't know that much about old cars. There, she would spend the day wandering the sidewalks, shopping, having coffee, a light lunch. No one knew how she fit into the once massive—but still rich and powerful—family, and she wasn't talking. She came into the diner sometimes while I was seated at the counter with my coffee and cigarettes. Always said hello, even knew my name—I had no idea how at the time—and sometimes we exchanged pleasant small talk. She always wore dull, colorless clothes that hung loosely on her, with her dark hair in a bun at the back of her head. Somewhat plain but with unblemished, creamy skin and a friendly smile. She cheerfully greeted everyone, but never went beyond small talk, like the weather, the election, the fact that there seemed to be fewer wolves howling around the mountain these days, that sort of thing. Later in the afternoon, that long, mean-looking car with its toothy chrome grill would come pick her up again and drive her away.

Most of the students at Hand of God were from wealthy families. The tuition was exorbitant, and included none of the many expenses that come with moving someplace new to go to school full time. The small percentage of students who did not come from money attended on scholarships and loans. Some of them were downright poor. You could always tell which students they were—the ones in the humiliating clothes who sat separately from everyone else in the cafeteria. I always sat with them. They were more fun. And far more accepting.

If my tuition indeed came from the Bollingers, what on earth had possessed them to send *me* to college? Except for my occasional empty exchanges with Amanda in the diner, I had never known or even met any of them. Had the decision to send me to Hand of God been a random one? Or had they been watching me, looking into my life with invisible eyes? It kind of gave me the creeps. But for Grandma's sake, I didn't question it.

I did not find Jesus at the College of the Hand of God. They talked about him a lot, had a lot of pictures of him hanging around, even had him out in front of the administration building on a twelve-foot cross, but I never saw any sign of him there. I had some good teachers, got a good education while I was there, if you don't count the creationist science classes. Unfortunately, it came with mandatory church attendance once a week and prayer meetings three times a week. On top of that, the reading material I could bring on campus was subject to restrictions. I had started reading for pleasure—and to forget my pain—during my long hospital stays. I had read everything I could get my hands on, and had not shed the habit since. But for bringing the wrong kind of books on campus, I could be subject to fines, or even expulsion. Science fiction, horror, mystery, anything even vaguely sexual—they were all prohibited. I might have been able to put up with the stiff rules and endless preaching—not just in church and prayer meetings, but in daily life as well, because I was seen as a troubled soul to be saved, and was adopted by many as a "project"—if it had not been for all the unsolicited explanations for what had happened to me. They started slowly at first. Once from the professor of my Bible class, again from one of the campus nurses, and from a couple of smiling, expensively-dressed students.

"It was God's will."

Referring, of course, to my face. At first, I was able to tell myself they weren't thinking, didn't realize exactly what they were saying. But after a while, I began to wonder why the hell they *didn't* realize exactly what they were saying. Weren't their mouths attached to their brains? Then one day, it became too much.

Pastor Knotts asked me to choose and read a passage of scripture in church before the congregation. It was a little honor now and then bestowed upon carefully selected students. So I picked out a couple of verses from the book of Matthew, and after I'd read them, I turned to leave the dais. Pastor Knotts grabbed my arm and pulled me back to the pulpit, put his arm around my shoulders.

"I'd like to introduce to our congregation today an extraordinary young man, and an exemplary student at Hand of God," Pastor Knotts said in his even, perfectly modulated voice. He sounded like a game show announcer giving a dramatic reading of a newspaper's obituaries. "His name is Andy Sayers and he comes into our loving fold after much hardship and pain."

I wanted to run from the building and never show my face there again. I wanted to strangle Knotts. I wanted to strangle myself. He went on and on and on, and his words melted together into a kind of psychedelic blur of humiliating sound, until he said:

"—of course, that it was God's will." Knotts turned to me with a long-toothed smile, reached out his hand, and I automatically shook it. "I would like to welcome you here to our mountain, Andy, and I want you to know—"

"Wait a second," I said, frowning. "Did…did you just say that this—" I pointed to my face. "—that what happened to my face, did you just say that was… *God's* will?"

His smile faltered as he dropped my hand, stumbled over a few words. "Well, uh, a*hem*, er, we all know the Bible promises that all things work together for—"

"You really believe that God *wanted* this to happen to me?"

The smile was gone and his posture became stiffer than usual—which I, until that moment, had thought to be physically impossible. "As *Christians,* Andrew, we believe that God has a purpose in everything he—"

I raised my voice. "Yes or no, do you believe this was God's will?"

His already creased face wrinkled even more and took on the look of a soft, rotting apple collapsing in on itself. His jaw clenched and he said, "Yes, we *do* believe that it was God's will, Andrew. Of *course* we do."

I spread my arms beseechingly and shouted, "Then why the fuck do you *worship* the sick bastard?"

Grandma's wail began the instant I said the word "fuck" and did not die out until shortly after I finished my question. I started across the dais, but stopped and turned back to him as a murmur grew into noisy chatter from the congregation. "I've been here almost a *year*!" I shouted. "Why the hell are you welcoming me *now*?"

Grandma let loose another long one as I went out a side door, down a hall and out the back. No more church for me. And no more College of the Hand of God. I sent President Morton a letter of thanks to be forwarded to my benefactor, and a letter explaining that I would not be returning to my classes. I did it all very quickly, before they could kick me out.

Grandma hasn't spoken to me since.

Mt. Crag was blanketed by a thick forest of green, punctuated by great craggy shelves of stone that jutted from its sides, hence its name. A year ago, a fire had swept over the north face of the mountain, the college side, but had been under control just as everyone in Pinecrest was getting ready to evacuate. It had left the ground and naked tree trunks black as night. For days after the last flames were extinguished, tendrils of smoke had risen slowly, like lazy ghosts, from that side of the mountain. Smoke hovered in the summer sky over the Village and the town for what seemed like an unnaturally long time, as if it had no intention of dissipating. Driving up the mountain was like driving through some nightmare landscape that had been created for a horror movie. Ever since the fire, people had been complaining about how ugly it was, how beautiful it used to be. But somehow, it had always looked that way to me, even before the fire.

It fit the holiday, though. A black, twisted Halloween forest with fangs of gray rock.

Near the half-way mark, the charred surroundings gave way to green. Once in Pinecrest, you couldn't tell anything was different. You couldn't tell it was Halloween, either. The holiday was not celebrated in The Village, was not even acknowledged. No carved pumpkins or black and orange crepe paper, not in a Village of fundamentalist Christians. The only thing out of the ordinary around the Village that Halloween were all the red, white, and blue VOTE BUSH/CHENEY and BUSH/CHENEY 2000 signs.

I drove by the college, which crept up a hillside, blocks of buildings at a time. The administration building and science building were all you could see of the school from the bottom. The rest of it disappeared into the trees. There was no doubt that it was there, however. Just behind the large granite sign at the foot of the hill, with CHRISTIAN COLLEGE OF THE HAND OF GOD carved into it, stood the college's pride and joy: a twelve-foot-tall wood carving of Jesus Christ on the cross. It had been carved in 1894 by Lawrence Bollinger and given to the brand new school as a gift. The years had not been kind to Jesus. That giant crucifix had long been the subject of pranks and acts of vandalism. During my first week as a student there, someone had dressed the dying savior in a fishing cap, sunglasses, and a white T-shirt with bold writing on the front: My dad's in heaven, and all I got was this lousy crucifixion. The perpetrator was caught and promptly expelled.

Bollinger. If you go into the Mount Crag Public Library and swing a dead cat—something they don't happen to encourage there—you'll hit a book with that name in it.

The family goes back to Columbus. They were thought to be among the first "hillbillies," which they had remained for a very long time. Until one of them stumbled onto some oil.

They were rich overnight. Just like the Clampetts. No one was sure how much of the mountainous land the Bollinger's owned, but it was a lot. Maybe all of it. Anything that happened in that area—including the long-ago building of a secluded Christian college—happened only with the permission of the Bollingers. The family had donated a lot of money to the college over the years, although no Bollinger had ever enrolled. They were everywhere, and yet, with the exception of Amanda, were never seen. Evidence of their existence, their wealth and influence, could be found at nearly every turn, but no one knew what they looked like. Their names appeared in books on local history, on memorial plaques, on a small theater for the performing arts in town, but the family itself remained invisible, locked up in their great, sprawling, mountainside home.

# Two

"Hi, Grandma," I said as I entered the living room.

She made a sound behind closed lips. That was all she'd been doing since I left school—making vaguely responsive noises, an occasional monosyllabic answer to a question. But we didn't talk anymore. She no longer sat down and asked how my day was, or asked me to taste things while she was cooking. I had let her down.

But I did not let that keep me from talking. I refused to play her little game and talked to her as if nothing had changed. Drove her nuts, I think.

"How's it going?" I asked, but I didn't wait for a response. "Did you meet with the Floral Committee this morning? Red said he saw you over at the church when he was towing a car earlier."

She nodded, rocking in her chair. In her large lap, she held an open Bible and some church literature, and held a magnifying glass in her right hand over the Bible. I once asked her why she didn't get a Bible with larger print, and she said, "Then the letters would be too big through my magnifying glass."

Scratchy church music played on her ancient record player, which she still called a phonograph. Piano and strings and some kind of flute. There was always music coming from somewhere in the Village, and it was always depressing and bloody and full of death.

Fortunately, I could not hear it from my apartment over the garage. It was my refuge. I had everything I needed there. A bed, all my books, a small refrigerator, which I kept locked, to keep beer cold and hidden from Grandma, and a television and VCR.

There was no cable in the Village because there was no demand for it. I had rigged an antenna up on the roof from my window, but it made little difference; reception had never been very good there. But when stations did come in, they were interesting and varied. Sometimes, there would be a period of a few days when I could pick up as many as a dozen channels. A few of them would play only old black-and-white shows, even with old black-and-white commercials, while others would broadcast in foreign languages.

Once, I found Sumo wrestling on one station and a gloomy, poorly shot cockfight on another. One station seemed to play nothing but old news footage about the assassination of President Kennedy.

"Don't worry about me for dinner, Grandma," I called from the kitchen as I poked around in the refrigerator. "I'm going down the hill to help with the Halloween celebration." I scooped some left-over bean-and-corn casserole onto a paper plate. "With a kill—er, um, somebody, y'know, killing people out there, they need enough people to keep the kids supervised and occu—"

I turned around and she was standing right there in front of me and it scared me so much, I yelped like a dog and dropped the casserole on the paper plate to the floor.

She hardly seemed to notice.

"You went to the funeral?" she asked, looking disapprovingly at the black jeans I wore with my coat and tie.

I took a deep breath and gave myself a moment to get my bearings again. "Yes. It was just a graveside service, but there were a lot of people there."

Grandma was pear-shaped and slightly stooped. Very grandmotherly. Until she started talking religion. She shook her head slowly and said, "It's the work of the devil, Andrew."

I had been waiting for that. I smiled and said, "I'm not helping the devil tonight, Grandma, I'm helping the kids."

She squinted through her glasses a moment, then clicked her tongue. "Not that, I'm not talking about *that*." Her dentures clacked together. "I'm talking about the killings. They're the work of the devil. Or maybe they're the work of God. Trying to test us, somehow. Trying to tell us something. Sometimes it's hard to tell the difference between the two." She reached out, closed a knobby, arthritic hand on my upper arm. "That's why we gotta be diligent, Andrew, honey. And that's why you never shoulda dropped out of school. You were meant to go to that school and learn God's word. There wasn't a single killing the whole time you were enrolled at Hand of God. No one went missing. No one just dropped off the face of God's earth like they never was. Everything was nice, and the only funeral was from *natural* causes."

I tried not to laugh. "Well, the stock market didn't crash, either, but that doesn't make me Alan Greenspan. Grandma, don't you think that's a little—"

"Wait till people start to see," she went on. "Wait till all your friends down the hill figure it out. They'll start to *suspect* you."

I let the laugh come that time and her hand dropped from my arm. "Grandma, my friends don't *think* that way!"

"Oh, yes, they do," she said as she turned and left the kitchen. "They just do it for the wrong side."

Either Grandma was suddenly losing her mind very quickly, or she was having one of her biblical brainstorms. Sometimes it was hard to tell the difference between the two.

When Grandma first took me into her care, I thought she seemed so sad because of what had happened to Mom, her daughter. As I got older, I saw my error. It wasn't what had happened to Mom that mattered, but how what had happened to Mom might look to everyone else. Grandma was embarrassed, humiliated among her people.

Somehow, Janine Sayers—my grandma—had failed in her effort to raise a good Christian girl in accordance with scripture and the tenets of her church. Instead, she had raised a troubled, angry girl who flew into rages, then became as loving as a kitten. A girl who quickly developed a drinking problem and moved to the city, where it grew worse, and where she was impregnated without the benefit of wedlock by some guy she met in a bar whose name she did not know.

I can remember times when my mom would hold me in her

arms and cover me with kisses. Times when she'd spin in circles laughing with me, our hands locked, until neither of us could stand up anymore. But she would change so quickly, become quiet and brooding, or enraged, or incoherent. And then she would drink. And drink, and drink.

I never resented her for any of her behavior, for the way she treated me sometimes. Grandma refuses to believe me, but I didn't even hold against my mom the fact that she had started the fire that burned my face, head, and neck so badly. Watching her twist and suffer at the whim of her illness—it had always been clear to me that she was sick—how could I feel anything for her but agonizing pity?

She had been drinking the night of the fire and had passed out on the sofa in the living room while I slept in my bed. She'd been smoking a cigarette at the time. The place was in flames when she coughed herself awake and ran from the apartment, down the steps and past the pool, screaming. Into the pool, dizzy. Later, she said she'd forgotten me, but I knew better. She'd just been drunk. One of the neighbors had pulled me out just before the fire trucks arrived.

Grandma showed up then and took over. I remember very little from that initial period after the fire—except for the pain, I remember that very well—and know only what Grandma has told me. I never saw my mother again. After her first visit to my bedside in the hospital, she went home and closed her teeth on the barrel of a gun. Killed herself.

I would go through those years of intensely painful operations and skin grafts once again if it would bring her back. Illness and all. It would be worth it just for those fleeting times when she was happy, and all was right with the world.

Living in the house in which Mom had grown up, I wondered how much of that torturing illness had been my mother's alone, and how much of it had been passed to her directly from her own mother, or how much was simply the result of being raised by her.

I had not given a moment of thought to a costume, so I quickly poked around in my closet and drawers for a few minutes before leaving to go down the mountain, looking for things that might be combined into a costume. My heart wasn't in it, so I didn't look long. Somehow, it did not feel right to dress up in a Halloween costume the evening of Carla's funeral.

It was still raining. The road that snaked down the mountain was dangerous in the rain. I had a great deal of respect for that road. It went down the mountain like a snake, curving sharply this way, that way. The downward-bound side of the road dropped sharply into jagged gray boulders around which a creek bubbled cheerfully. I had hiked along that creek. There were a lot of broken pieces of cars scattered around down there, and a lot of people had been hurt, crippled, and killed among them. I had no intention of being one of them. Besides, there was little chance I would be speeding down the hill, never mind up, in my blue 1972 Volkswagen Beetle. That car hadn't sped anywhere in a long time.

The rain made the blackness of the burned forest gleam in my headlights. It looked unnatural, menacing, and I could never shake the feeling, as I drove through the charred landscape, that it was watching me.

Although it was raining hard, the Halloween celebration would take place as planned. Up and down the main street of Mount Crag—which was called, coincidentally, Main Street—children would gather to play organized games on the covered sidewalks and receive prizes from the shops that lined the street. Merchants had agreed to stay open past closing time to participate. Just as they had for a few years now. Every precaution had been taken.

Carla Firth wasn't the first young woman to show up dead. And she wasn't the first to die that way—slashed and badly bitten, partially gutted. She was only the first in a while.

# Three

"You didn't wear a costume?" Carrie asked. She looked broken-hearted.

I shrugged. "I just wasn't in the mood, you know? The funeral and all."

She nodded sympathetically as she poured my coffee at the counter. "Well, it's not like I went all out."

Carrie was dressed as a gypsy, with necklaces and bracelets that dangled and clattered.

"You look great!" I said, and meant it. She always looked great. Except in her eyes, where she always looked a little wounded.

"It's a wonder I got as much of this thrown together as I did this morning," she said, cleaning behind the counter. "Keith fell down the steps in front of our house and slammed his head on the concrete walk. I took him down to the walk-in clinic and he had to have some stitches. Stayed home from school today."

"Is he all right?"

"Yeah, he's fine. He's decided to make use of the stitches in his forehead and dress as the Frankenstein monster. Mom's going to bring them over in time for the parade. Wanna go trick-or-treating with us?"

"Sure." By trick-or-treating, she meant going from shop to shop up and down

Main Street. Sometimes they got candy, and sometimes they got gift certificates or even toys. The merchants had come to compete with one another in giving out the best candy, the most unusual gifts. And the kids got a whole lot of advertising flyers with their Tootsie Rolls and Butterfingers, which were handed off, of course, to Mom and Dad.

"Well, you'll have to wear *something.* The boys would be disappointed if you didn't."

"Do I look like somebody who needs to come up with a scary costume for Halloween?" I asked with a smile.

Carrie jerked as if I had reached across the counter and poked her in the stomach. "How could you say such a thing, Andy?" She sounded shocked, even hurt.

"Just a joke, Carrie."

"But that's a terrible thing to say about yourself. That kind of thinking damages your self-esteem, and you—"

I laughed and said, "Have you been watching *Oprah,* or something?"

She slapped my arm with a hand towel.

"I've got plenty of self-esteem, Carrie," I assured her quietly. "But I've also got a sense of humor. Sometimes I need to laugh about it as much as some people need to stare at it."

Carrie folded her arms and sighed. "Sometimes you sound two or three times your own age."

"What's that mean?"

"I'm not really sure. I'm tired. You want the special tonight, Andy? Pork chops with rice—oh, wait, you hate pork, don't you? Okay, what would you like?"

Carrie used to do nearly everything but cook in the diner. She had inherited the Pantry Shelf from her father; she had played and worked there since she could remember. She had been running it since her father had a heart attack, she and Gustav, the cook, a monolith of a man who spoke with an impenetrable Eastern European accent, and who had worked for her father since the diner first opened for business.

In the past year, she had hired a couple of waitresses, both single mothers like herself. She no longer waited tables, but she was all over the diner, never holding still, pouring coffee or operating the register, busing tables or cleaning up messes, and always chatting with customers, making them feel welcome. And yet, she always had time to take my order.

She went to the window and shouted my order to

Gustav, whose reply sounded like someone breaking granite. Miraculously, Carrie understood what he said and responded. Sometimes when she did that, I wondered if she simply gave a random response to make everyone *think* she understood him, when in fact, she was as stumped by Gustav's accent as the rest of us.

Carrie returned to the counter and rested her arms on it, leaned forward. "I'd planned to go to the funeral, but I was too busy with Keith. Were there a lot of people?"

I nodded. "Especially for a graveside service in the rain. I didn't stay very long."

"Her poor parents. I ache for those people."

"Yeah. I'm sure they're real upset because Carla won't be finishing college."

"Oh, c'mon, Andy, have a little compassion. They're suffering right now."

I shrugged, said no more about it. I'd known Carla's parents from church when I attended Hand of God. Her father was a deacon who would tell you all about the many illnesses and hardships with which God had been testing him his whole life until your head split open like a macheted melon. And the whole time he talked, his wife would be nodding her head silently, up and down, nodding and nodding. When it came to their daughter, all they cared about was that she get excellent grades in college and go to church every Sunday. Nothing else mattered to them. Normally, I was a very compassionate person—at least, I'd always thought so—but I had spent just enough time with Mr. and Mrs. Firth for compassion to come very slowly.

"I bet it eats at them," Carrie said quietly, staring at my coffee. "Even in their sleep."

"What eats at them?"

Her voice dropped to a whisper. "Wondering...y'know... who."

I shook my head. "Who killed their daughter, you mean?"

Carrie blinked a couple times and her upper lip started to curl, but did not. "Yeah, that's what I meant."

I folded my arms on the counter and leaned close to her, whispered, "Then why didn't you say it?"

"I guess I'm just not very comfortable talking about…Well, about death."

"Nobody in this town is," I said, still whispering. "Every time this happens, everybody talks about it like somebody moved out of town. Left the country. Not like somebody was killed. *Again.* Ripped apart in the woods by some…animal, some monster that will just do it again later because nothing's done."

Carrie frowned. "Did you hear something about it being an animal?"

"No, I meant the person doing the—never mind."

"Well, I heard something." She stood up straight, brushed a strand of her chestnut hair back from her forehead, then came around the counter, sat beside me and leaned close. Whatever she had heard, she wanted no one else to hear it.

There was a quiet middle-aged couple at one booth, unfamiliar, probably just passing through. Old Pete was in his usual corner by the front window, a one-eyed World War II veteran who looked like he was made of old leather. He came to the diner every day. Otherwise, it was empty. Only one waitress, Lucy, was working. Everyone was busy preparing for the Halloween festivities.

"A little while after the lunch crowd cleared out," Carrie said, "Chief Ledbetter came in with that new expert they brought up here from the city."

"The forensics guy?" I asked.

She nodded. "Retired. An old guy, but apparently sharp. They whispered to each other over coffee and pie so no one could hear, but when you've worked in a diner as long as I have, you learn to eavesdrop under any conditions. I could probably eavesdrop on a conversation in sign language outside at night in the middle of a blizzard, if I had to."

"What'd they say?"

"The old man did most of the talking," Carrie whispered. "He said it wasn't a person."

"What do you mean?"

"Whoever did that to Carla Firth? It wasn't a who. This guy says it couldn't be human, that it's an animal, most likely a bear.

And he thinks the same thing happened to the others. The ones he reviewed, anyway."

The bear theory had enjoyed a couple of periods of popularity in the town, but they had been brief, and a long time ago.

"Then it's a bear with some very specific tastes," I said.

"Yeah, that's what I thought. Young, blonde, and pretty. Anyway, Chief Ledbetter said he had a hard time believing it was a bear, or any animal, but just in case, he would quietly organize a hunt to track it down and kill it if it's out there."

"Haven't they done that before?"

"Twice, I think, but it was a long time ago. The chief sounded pretty doubtful. But what if the old guy's right? Wouldn't it be nice if all we have to do is kill a bear to make it stop?"

Lucy brought my dinner. I took a few bites, then asked, "Have you ever wondered why there haven't been more experts up here from the city? Or why no reporters have covered this? How come it hasn't shown up on *Dateline* or *20/20*?"

She shrugged one shoulder. "The killings are too far apart," she whispered. "The killer's too slow."

"But how many over the years?"

"I don't know. I haven't kept track."

"That's what I mean. Nobody here keeps track, they just act like it's no big deal, comes with the territory. The leaves turn in autumn, the fruit trees blossom in spring.

"And oh, yeah, we found another dead blonde girl with her insides spilled all over the ground in the woods. Chief Ledbetter goes through the same motions each time. No reporters come to gather the facts." I shook my head. "I'm glad I'm getting out of here."

"What? You're leaving? When?"

"I'm not sure. Sometime soon."

"When did you decide this?"

"Today."

"Where will you go?"

"Anywhere but here. I've saved a little money. Enough to get me somewhere."

"What about your grandma?"

"She'll probably be glad to see my heathen ass go."

Carrie put an arm around my shoulders. "Andy, you can't go. What am I gonna do without you here?"

I smiled. "You can always pack up the kids and come with me. Wouldn't you like to get out of this town? Go someplace where they don't have bears and retired forensic experts?"

She put her elbows on the countertop and her face in her hands. "This is too depressing. Can we talk about something else?"

I continued eating.

"You going to the grown-up party afterward?" Carrie asked.

"I don't know."

"Oh, c'mon, it'll be fun. You're old enough now, remember? You were still too young to drink at last year's party."

"I drank anyway."

"Yeah, but this is the first year it counts. Besides, Rick and Daisy always throw a great Halloween party at the bar."

The bar was the Rusty Nail, just two doors down from the diner. There was another bar in the old Mount Crag Hotel at the other end of Main Street, but it was patronized mostly by people who were just passing through, and there were never that many of those. All the locals went to the Rusty Nail.

"We've still got to find you a costume," Carrie said. "The boys will be here soon and they'll be disappointed if you're not wearing *something*."

"Okay. But something simple. A hat, or something. Okay?"

"Okay." She smiled and kissed the top of my head as she walked away.

Everything seemed too dark and ominous for me to enjoy Halloween, a holiday I usually relished because it gave me an excuse to cover my face. Another dead girl in the ground. Gathering children on Main Street again instead of taking them trick-or-treating from house to house at the foot of the mountain. All to protect them from whatever was out there. A bear? Maybe, maybe not. I reminded myself to look in next week's Mount Crag *Sentinel* for the details Carrie had overheard in the diner. But I doubted I would see them. Carrie found a pair of purple antennae that bobbed on springs attached to a headband, which she put on my head. It made her happy, and that made me feel a little better.

The Chamber of Commerce put on a small Halloween parade just before the sun disappeared. The drizzle had become little more than a mist by then, as if the frowning, angry sky had decided to give us a break. The gutters ran with brown water and puddles spread here and there over the street. The parade just danced around them. There were monsters and clowns, a fairy Godmother and a couple of bunny rabbits. All the costumes were homemade but impressive. Even Mayor Tucker had dressed up to take part in the parade. He zigzagged along the wet street, growling at the children, who squealed and laughed. He wore a bulky, furry bear costume.

It was a lot like last year's Halloween celebration, and the others before it. But it was always fun to see. The children had a great time, and in spite of all the complaining some of them did, so did the adults.

The thing that was different about that night—the thing that had never, ever happened to me before—came later.

# Four

It was all over in a couple of hours. The adults took the children home with their candy and prizes, leaving behind the pumpkins in the shop windows, carved faces somewhat withered by the heat of the candles that had been burning inside them.

Crepe paper and artificial cobwebs sagged as if from exhaustion. Having already arranged babysitters, most of the adults returned almost immediately and went to the bar, in costume and ready to party.

Carrie's boys went home with their grandma, Carrie's mother, who lived with them, after promising their mom they would not watch any monster movies that were *too* scary. The diner had a large bathroom in back with a shower, and Carrie used it to shower and put on makeup. I did not feel much like going to a party, but Carrie did not want to go alone, so I went with her, wearing my antennae and holding my umbrella over both of us against the slowly increasing rain.

The party was already well underway when we got there. Rick and Dixie had brought in a band from somewhere out of town, and they were playing "The Purple People Eater" when we arrived. A few people were dancing, and others quickly joined them. Smoke filled the place. It was the only thing that bothered me about the bar. I didn't mind that anyone was smoking, I was never one of *those* people. It wasn't the smoking I didn't like, but the smoke itself. There was a tiny part of me deep inside that started screaming with terror every time I saw all that smoke hovering ominously in the air. It brought back memories.

Carrie knew better than to ask me to dance. I had the rhythm of a bowl of dirt and was far too self-conscious to get on a dance floor. I had a beer or two. Or three. Occasionally picked at the bowls of nuts and candy that were set out all over the place. Ninety minutes after Carrie and I arrived, the bar was deafening and had a capacity crowd, with late-comers trying hard to catch up on drinks. The people of Mount Crag did not party often, but when they did, they partied hard.

I played darts with a couple of guys I'd met while enrolled at Hand of God, both colossally drunk. They were second year students who, through some miracle, had not yet been kicked off the campus. I played a game of pool with Red Prater, who ran the autobody shop over by the park. He was about as good at the game as I, so it took a lot longer than it should have because we were both lousy, but he finally beat me. I was walking back to the bar when she came in.

She hung her umbrella over my jacket on one of the coat racks by the door as she entered, peeled off her coat. It was snowy white, with an enormous black fur collar. I recognized it as monkey-fur—or something that was supposed to look like monkey-fur—which used to be very popular back in the twenties, and she was clearly a "flapper" from that era. The sleeveless, beaded dress beneath was red and black, with a low neckline and a scarf hemline. There were a lot of lines involved, all of them very pleasing. She held a black, beaded clutch in one hand and a lit cigarette in a long, slender, black-and-silver holder between the first two fingers of the other. She wore stockings, black, low-heeled shoes, and a beautiful jeweled mask covered the top half of her face, with a fan of red and black feathers on each side that obscured the rest. The costume was probably as shocking in that bar as it might have been in its own day.

When the woman walked in, there were a lot of double-takes, and more than a few triple-takes. There probably were some arguments on the way home that night, as well, involving the length of time some boyfriends and husbands spent gazing at the stranger in red. I could tell by the looks on the faces of a couple of women that their husbands would not be getting any candy that Halloween. But then I did a double-take of my own as I reached the bar.

The flapper was looking directly at me, even coming toward me. Her blood-red, bee-stung lips smiled without parting. She held the cigarette up, elbow cocked, and threw her hips into her walk. Her nails matched the red of her dress.

The band did not stop playing, of course, but voices fell away like cardboard ducks at a carnival shooting gallery. Not all of them, but enough to make a dip in the sound level.

*Do I know her?* I wondered as she came toward me, her smile growing. She did not look even a little familiar. As far as I could tell, I had never seen her before. But she was coming straight for me, and a lot of people were watching her. Soon, they would be watching me, too. I hated being watched.

"Well, aren't you adorable," she said in a low, smoky voice, pointing her cigarette at my antennae. She scooted the next stool closer to me, then perched herself on it and leaned close. Her beaded dress chittered with each movement, and she smelled of lilacs. "What planet are *you* from?"

I was right. They were all watching us. When I glanced at them, every face turned away.

"I come from the planet of people who need another beer," I said, smiling, but my lips trembled because I was so nervous. I waved at Rick, who was laughing at somebody's joke at the other end of the bar.

"'Nother beer, Andy?" he asked.

I nodded.

"Can I buy you a drink?" I asked.

"That's very sweet of you, but I don't drink. In fact, no one in my family drinks or smokes. They never have."

My eyes moved to the cigarette in the long holder, then back to her deep brown eyes behind the mask.

"Except for me," she said finally, reluctantly. "But only sometimes. On special occasions. Very rarely." She paused a moment, then leaned closer and whispered into my ear, "Just don't tell my father, okay?"

Then she laughed and touched my wrist, and I was so surprised by that touch, I nearly fell off the stool. To cover, I laughed, too, then asked, "How about a ginger ale, then?"

"A ginger ale! What a *fabulous* idea! I'll take you up on that."

When Rick came with my beer, I put some money on the bar and said, "A ginger ale, too, Rick." He nodded. I was surprised to see him smile at the woman.

"Great costume this year," he said to her. "Probably your best."

Rick knew her. I wondered if the others had been looking at her out of curiosity or familiarity. I took a couple swallows of courage and asked, "Excuse me, but, um, do I know you?"

She shook her head slightly. When she spoke, I watched her pillowy red lips form the words slowly and perfectly, saw the quick flick of the tongue within, then the smile.

"No, not really."

Applause erupted when the band finished an old Hank Williams foot-stomper.

The lead singer and bass player started telling a joke and the chatter died down as everyone listened.

When I turned back to the woman, she was sipping her ginger ale. "Very sweet of you to buy me a drink," she said, leaning close to me again. "It's delicious."

I was too uncomfortable to continue engaging in casual conversation. I extended my hand and said, "I'm Andy Sawyer."

With the cigarette holder clamped beneath her teeth, she took my hand between both of hers and stroked it in a way that sent crackling tendrils of electricity directly to my genitals. "Of course you are," she said.

The singer's joke got more groans than laughs, and applause broke out as the band started to play again. The woman removed her cigarette butt from the holder, stabbed it into an ashtray on the bar, set the holder beside her drink. She turned to me with mouth open, gently pressed a palm against my chest. "This *song*!" she squealed. "I *love* this song!" It was the old Righteous Brothers hit, "That Loving Feeling." She declared, "We absolutely *must* dance!"

My shoulders dropped. I remained seated as she stood. She started to walk away, assuming, I suppose, that I was at her heels. When she realized I was not, she spun around and came back.

"Andy, honey, this is *not* a dance-alone song," she said.

I looked over my shoulder at the dance floor. "Looks pretty crowded," I said.

She leaned against me from behind and her breasts pressed to my back. Her lips touched my ear as she whispered, "Fine, then." Her right hand slid across my right thigh and between my legs, lingered there a moment, then slid down to my knee and pulled.

The stool's seat turned until I faced her. She smiled, took my hands, and said, "We'll do it right here." Then pulled me off the stool with a sudden, and surprisingly powerful, jerk.

Next thing I knew, her body was making slow movements against mine. Movements that were quickly becoming embarrassing for me.

When she felt my erection, she asked in my ear, "Is that the mother ship signaling you, spaceman, or are you just glad to see me?"

I could not reply. I was embarrassed, but not as much as I would have been without a few beers in me. The feathers on her mask tickled my face, and I considered asking her to remove it, but she spoke first.

"You are a very tense young man, Andy," she said as her tongue flicked over my earlobe. "You need to relax. Have a good time. You know that? It's Halloween." She pulled away from me, leaned toward the bar and called, "Hey, Ricky! A Long Island iced tea for the gentleman." Then we were together again, swaying. "What do you usually do on Halloween?"

I ran my tongue around in my dry mouth. "Nothing much to do but come here."

She kissed me—a quick, soft, brush of her lips against mine, then looked into my eyes for a reaction. I have no idea what she saw, but she must have liked it because she kissed me again, longer than before. Her tongue opened my lips with gentle, coaxing pressure.

I had never been with a woman before. I was very realistic about it, I knew my chances. I suspected it would happen one day, sooner or later, but I wasn't holding my breath waiting for it. I had heard from several people there was a whorehouse in the hills east of town, and I had considered trying to find it, but had never gotten around to it. I was too afraid of being turned away. However, that would be a marked improvement over "It was God's will." More honest, anyway.

As excited as I was while we danced—if it could be called dancing—I knew without a sliver of doubt that nothing would happen between myself and the strange, nameless woman beyond what was happening at that moment. But that made it no less exciting, and it did not keep me from enjoying her affection.

She whispered in my ear, "Have you ever fucked in a graveyard?"

I cleared my throat. "Um…no."

"That sounds like a Halloween kind of thing to do, doesn't it?" The tip of her tongue slowly ran down the outer edge of my ear, firing needles of sensation all the way to my nipples. "And it's Halloween, right?" Her tongue slid up the back of my ear, from bottom to top. It felt like it was wrapping around my ear, about to swallow it, then it was gone. My breathing had changed and my knees felt weak, and something warm and wet touched the back of my neck.

I spun around quickly with a startled grunt and my hand went to my neck, which was wet. But there was no one standing behind me or hurrying away with the slinking jog of a practical joker.

"Your iced tea is here," the woman said.

She was already returning to her stool. I joined her. My heart was firing heavy artillery in my chest, trying to start a war with the rest of my body, as I stared at the tall, fat glass filled with a dark, toxic mixture of gin, vodka, tequila, rum, sour mix, and triple sec.

During one of my many hospital stays, I'd found a book on the dayroom shelf called *The Fun Guide to Bartending* and read it. It was an unlikely book for a hospital dayroom, but I had memorized the ingredients of most of the drinks covered, and for some reason, remembered them still.

"I thought you said you don't drink," I said. I had a little difficulty with my tongue and realized I was feeling the beer. Now

I had the world champion of mixed drinks in front of me.

"I don't, darling."

"But you ordered me a Long Island ice tea? You just...know drinks?"

"Oh, I know *lots* of things," she whispered as she leaned over and kissed me again, placed a cool hand on my cheek. Then she continued sipping her ginger ale.

It hit me so hard, I almost slapped my forehead with my palm, like those people in the V-8 commercials.

*She's an idiot,* I thought. *She thinks my face is a mask, or makeup, some kind of Halloween costume. Which means she's an idiot. Possibly retarded.*

The most liquor I'd ever had was a couple of sips of whisky, which I hadn't cared for. But the iced tea was sweet and had only the slightest alcoholic taste.

"Drink up, spaceman," she said. "The sooner you finish that drink, the sooner we can get out of here."

"Get out of here?"

She laughed, leaned close and put her hand on my thigh again, her mouth to my ear. "And go fuck in the graveyard, silly."

I surprised myself with a loud laugh. "What? You've got to be kidding."

"It's Halloween!" she said cheerfully with a grin.

I laughed again, took another swallow of my drink. It was good, so I took another.

"You mean, you really want to go down to the cemetery and—"

"Not *that* cemetery." She leaned closer again, slowly closing the gap between us as she spoke. "Not the one here in town, silly. I'll take you to a graveyard you've never seen before. In a place you've never been."

I knew as she kissed me again that I would do it if she really wanted to, even in the pouring rain.

"Hi, Amanda," Carrie said behind me.

I jumped as I turned to Carrie, who was smiling at the woman.

"Carrie!" she said. "You look *deliciously* exotic. Are you telling fortunes tonight?"

"I'm so tired, I can barely tell what time it is." She turned to me, put a hand on my shoulder. "I'm going home, Andy. You gonna stick around for a while?"

"Do you need a ride?" I asked.

"No."

I turned to Amanda, and then I realized the significance of that name. "Amanda *Bollinger*?" I asked. "*Miss* Bollinger?" I blinked several times as I looked at her, and I saw it, finally. But her voice was different, deeper, and my God, she was beautiful, not the plain woman I was accustomed to seeing in the diner. And she'd just had her tongue in my mouth!

"Who on *earth* did you think I was?" she asked.

"Well, I-I-I…I *asked* if I knew you."

"And I answered truthfully that you do not. But *that* is going to change tonight."

She turned to Carrie. "We're going for a Halloween ride."

Carrie grinned at me. "That's great."

I quickly said, "But, um, Miss Bollinger, I came with—"

"If you call me that again, I will have to punish you," she said playfully.

"See, the thing is, I came here with Carrie, and—"

"Excuse me, Amanda, but can I borrow him for a second?" Carrie said as she clutched my elbow.

"Of course, of course."

Carrie led me through the crowded bar to the front. Stopped beside the entrance and took her coat off the long rack on the wall. "You don't have to worry about me, Andy, really."

"Then just *say* you need a ride, okay? So I can get out of here?"

She looked at me with utter disbelief. "Are you insane?"

"No, but I seriously think *she* might be."

"Andy, think of who you're talking about, here. It's not like she's a total stranger, or anything."

"Yes, it's *exactly* like she's a total stranger."

"Look, Andy, I don't know how you could possibly miss it, but I think she really likes you. Now, have fun, dammit." She put on her coat and grabbed her umbrella, kissed me on the cheek, and disappeared out the door.

When I returned to the bar, Amanda stood and said, "Take another drink, and then we have to go."

"We *have* to go?"

"Yes. Right away."

"Why?"

She smiled. "Because I'm already wet."

# Five

Amanda Bollinger drove like a madwoman. What made it worse was the fact that she was driving my Beetle, singing along loudly with an old Blue Oyster Cult song on the radio, feathered mask in her lap. The Beetle wasn't much, but it was all I had, and I told her several times to slow down, take it easy, it wasn't a Ferrari.

On the way to my parked car, I had discovered my keys were not in my jacket pocket. I told her to wait, I had to go back in and get them, but she laughed and hooked her arm in mine, jangled my keys from her other hand.

"I've got them," she'd said. "You're in no condition to drive, and even if you were, you haven't a *clue* where we're going."

I had my seatbelt on—Grandma had nagged me into the habit, until it became second-nature—and clutched the dashboard with my right hand as she raced around sharp curves through the rain. The windshield wipers slapped back and forth rapidly, unable to keep up with the furious strafing of my heart. We were going around the mountain rather than up Mt. Crag Pass, the road that led to the Village. After about thirty or forty minutes on the road, the fire-blackened side of the mountain was behind us.

Lightning flashed in the eastern sky in great sheets, turning the night the dim gray of an old silent film, followed by distant thunder that was muffled further by the sound of the rain hitting the car.

Amanda made a sharp right turn directly into the dark and smothering woods that went up the mountain.

"*Hey*!" I cried as the tires crunched over gravel and the car hit a ditch so hard that, had I not been wearing my seatbelt, the top of my head would have slammed into the bug's ceiling. As we humped and jostled over uneven ground, going much too fast, I cried out again, this time purely in fear. I slapped my other hand onto the dashboard and held on tight with both, expecting to have my spine wrapped around a tree at any moment.

A second later, we were on smooth pavement again, going uphill. The headlights cut through the rain to reveal a road hidden among the trees, wide enough for only one vehicle at a time. It cut steeply up the mountain, and just ahead it disappeared around a sharp curve.

"Hairpin!" Amanda shouted in much the same way a golfer might shout, "Fore!" as she pressed her foot on the accelerator.

Terrified, I let fly a stream of angry obscenities as she took the curve too fast. I felt the Beetle's worn tires lose their grip on the wet pavement and slip and slide dangerously for a moment. Then we were on a straight stretch again, climbing the mountain, and Amanda was laughing loud and hard.

"Why aren't you having fun?" she asked with great enthusiasm.

"Because I'm too scared of *dying* to have fun!" I replied angrily.

"Oh, I just adore driving. Unfortunately, I don't get to do it very often."

"Yeah, I can tell."

Her laughter was close to a shriek. "I can tell that *you*, my dear, are quite desperately in need of a good fuck."

She took the car off the road again, but this time she slowed down first, so it was not quite as dramatic as before. The headlight beams spilled over an even narrower road of mud, but although the high beams were on, they did not shine very far. The night was even darker beneath the mountain's tree. I had no idea where we were.

I was still shaken by the life-threatening ride, worried about my car's well-being.

Amanda's driving had made me angry. But I was still achingly hard, had been since we left the bar. I could not believe what I was doing. I was not even *sure* what I was doing.

A waist-high stone fence appeared beside the muddy path, and Amanda pulled over and parked the car beside it. She killed the engine and turned to me, grinning.

"Shall we?" she asked.

"It's raining," I said.

"Awwww," she said mockingly as she reached over and pinched my left cheek.

"Does him not wanna get wet?"

I sighed, smirked. "I can't tell if you're trying to seduce me or piss me off, Miss Bollinger."

She wagged a finger at me chidingly. "Ah-ah-*ah*. Didn't I say I would punish you if you called me that again?" She leaned toward me. "The first part of your punishment..."

Slid her hand over the bulge in my jeans. "...is to get out of the car..." Kissed me quickly and hard, sucking my tongue into her mouth and the breath from my lungs. "...and get soaking... fucking... *wet*." Then she was out the door and into the night.

I kept a Maglite flashlight on the floor behind my seat, one of the big ones, about twenty inches long with the beefy heft of a dangerous weapon. I opened the door and got out, pushed the seat-back forward, leaned into the car, and felt for the flashlight in the darkness.

Something skimmed the back of my head and landed in the back seat with the rattle of a thousand teeth. I recognized the sound, knew what it was even though I could see no more than a ghostly, shapeless heap of darkness against the pale upholstery.

She had thrown her beaded dress into the car.

Amanda stood next to me, naked except for shoes, stockings, and black garters.

She closed the car door, moved close and put her arms around my waist.

"The rest of your punishment," she whispered, "is to fuck me."

I passed a trembling hand lightly over the smooth skin of her back, already wet from the rain, as she nibbled on my neck. "That's a punishment?" I asked as I pulled back and peeled my jacket off, tossed it into the car.

I could feel her smile against my skin. "It can be." She took my hand, pulled me into the night. "I know just the place."

I turned on the flashlight as she led me through a narrow gap in the stone fence.

"What's *that* for?" she asked disdainfully.

"For...light."

"Turn it off. We don't need it."

"Well, if you don't mind, I'd like to leave it on till we get where we're going, because I can't *see* anything."

"What's to see? You see one graveyard, you've seen 'em all."

I wanted to see her more than anything else. I was certain there was nothing plain about her without her clothes, and I wanted some light to see for myself. But I was so embarrassed, I was surprised I could speak clearly. If it had not been for the Long Island iced tea, there was no way I could have gone through with it.

*Did she know that?* I wondered, with the taste of her fresh in my mouth.

Not quite as steady on my feet as usual, I asked Amanda if she would slow down a little, and she did. I could hear her shoes slopping in the mud.

"I hope you didn't rent that costume," I said.

"Belonged to my great-grandmother."

Gravestones stood like soldiers all around us. We serpentined around them and the flashlight's beam slid over their old, chipped marble surfaces chiseled with weathered letters and cherubs, praying hands and crucifixes. Amanda was right—if you've seen one, you've seen 'em all.

She led me to a rectangular slab of stone flat on the ground, about six feet long, three wide. I couldn't read the words in the rain, but there were a lot of them. It looked like a whole family had been buried there.

Amanda snaked into the beam of light, stretched out on the slab on her back, propped on her elbows, one knee cocked. She smiled up at me. Even though the flashlight's beam was not flattering light, she was beautiful. Until lightning flashed. It turned her already pale skin a harsh white, marbled it with a bruise-like purplish-blue. As she lay on the gravestone of a dead family. A shudder went through me and I took a step back.

"I-I'm sorry," I said. "But I can't...I just can't do this. It's too... it's too..."

"Sick?" she asked, still smiling, and I nodded. She reached out and grabbed the waist of my jeans and said, "Oh, darling, we haven't even *started* yet," as she pulled me down to her.

My nod had been inaccurate. Yes, it was probably sick to have sex on a gravestone, but that was not what made me want to go. I was unable to recognize it at the time—probably because of all the beer I'd drunk and the Long Island iced tea I had not quite finished—but it was probably the same feeling a young mother gets when the house becomes too quiet. It was the dead weight of the silence right after a pondful of frogs have all stopped croaking at the same instant. It was one of the many parts of the brain we do not yet understand pounding helplessly on the wall to alert the relatively small part we do.

How I wish I had shown more respect for that shudder. But once she had me down there on the cold, wet stone, it was already too late.

Friends have told me stories of their first times, the stories of their friends' first times. I have only heard one that sounded like a truly erotic experience, and I didn't believe a word of it. Most of them were stories of discomfort, embarrassment, and, as in the case of a guy I met at Hand of God, a senior named Oliver Hodel, life-threatening danger. A friend of Oliver's oldest sister—a *married* friend—decided to make a man out of him, and told him so. At her place, with her psychotic husband on his way home from work expecting to find a hot meal ready. Oliver was seventeen, she was thirty-three, and her two kids were playing with friends next door. On top of that, she was on her period.

And she was a gusher. He barely got out of the house unseen by her arriving husband and had to go out the bathroom window to do it. But it didn't end there. When Oliver's mother did the laundry the next day, she saw his bloody underwear and screamed as if she had discovered a corpse in the washing machine. When an explanation was demanded, Oliver, a nervous wreck over the whole thing, could come up with nothing but the truth, and was grounded until he turned eighteen.

I like that story, and whenever the subject of first times comes up, I enjoy telling it. No matter how old I live to be, I will never tell the story of my own first time during one of those conversations. Never.

I put the flashlight on the large gravestone beside us, still shining. The rain was cold, and the stone was colder. My clothes were soaked through, and it was an effort to get my jeans halfway down. I never had a chance to take them all the way off. She popped a couple of buttons off my shirt before I could unbutton the rest. I never managed to take it off, just left it open. She moved her hands around beneath my shirt, grabbed my erection—I assumed she had reached down between us—and pulled me into her.

Until that night, the only person who had ever touched my face since the fire, besides doctors and nurses, was Carrie. She was the only person who had ever given me a friendly peck on the cheek or playful tweak of my chin. She would never know how grateful I would always be for those brief but warm moments of affectionate contact. I could not feel her touch on my scarred and grafted skin, but I could feel the pressure of her hand, her lips. My mom had not lived long enough to touch my face, and while Grandma had been quite affectionate when I was a boy, she'd carefully avoided touching me above the shoulders.

Amanda, on the other hand, seemed to be unaware of the fact that I had been burned. Holding my head firmly between both hands as I moved inside her, she kissed me passionately, moaned as she filled my mouth with her tongue until I was afraid I would gag. Then she kissed my face repeatedly, licked it, sucked on my earlobe as her breathing came faster and faster, along with mine.

I forgot about the rain, the cold, where we were. They were all melted away by the heat between us. I tried to slow down because I knew I would finish soon, and I did not want to, not yet, not so quickly. But she would not let me. She reached down and squeezed my buttocks, dug her fingernails in and pushed me into her hard and fast as she sucked on my neck, licked it.

I was so close to exploding and didn't want to, didn't want to pop off in less than a minute like the virgin I was. Her tongue slid over my throat, back over the side of my neck, farther and farther back. Over the tendons at the base of my skull.

I opened my eyes. Saw that her head was still right beside mine. As her tongue crept beneath the back of my shirt collar to moisten the skin between my shoulder blades.

My heart seemed to stop beating when I stopped moving. I froze for a moment, wondering if the beer and hard liquor were making some of my synapses misfire. But no, it was there, all right. Her tongue. Licking my back.

I pulled my head back, caught a blurred flash of quick, glistening movement between our faces. Amanda smiled up at me as I started to pullout, to get up on my knees, but she wrapped her fingers around my penis and squeezed hard, holding me there.

Except her hands were on my shoulders.

As she squeezed my erection harder, still smiling, something curled beneath my scrotum and firmly cupped my testicles.

I heard my scream before I knew it was coming from me. Next thing I knew, I was off her, crawling away from her, crab-like on my back, trying to get to my feet with my soaked jeans bunched around my knees, and in the shadowy glow of the flashlight I saw, once again, another whip of movement. This time between her thighs.

Still lying on the stone, Amanda laughed like a little girl who had just tied the laces of both my shoes together. Then she got up.

On my feet, I backed away from her as I pulled up my jeans, buttoned them. But she did not come toward me. Instead, she turned and ran in the opposite direction, arms spread at her sides, laughing as she skipped like a happy child every few steps, until she was swallowed up by the darkness.

I quickly buttoned my shirt, picked up the flashlight. I was shivering, but not from the cold or rain. I could not feel either. My shivering came from fear, confusion. My scrotum had shriveled and was still tingling from the touch of…something.

There was another corpse-white flash of distant lightning, and its glow filtered through the trees in an instant of dizzying patterns. In that moment, I saw her pale back as she danced around gravestones and through another gap in the stone fence, out of the cemetery.

"You're no fun!" she called over her shoulder.

I shone the flashlight ahead of me and went after her, shouting, "Wait! Amanda! Where are you *going*?"

I heard what sounded like her shoes clapping on wooden planks. Then a loud creak. She laughed again, but the high, musical sound was cut short by the slam of a door.

Hurrying through the small cemetery, something struck me about the gravestones, something odd enough to make me slow to a stop. I passed the flashlight beam back and forth slowly over the stones around me. It took a moment before I could identify the oddity.

They were all so close together. Too close. Looking closer, I realized they were very small graves. At first, I thought it might be a pet cemetery, but something in the lower part of my guts told me that was not the case. I went to one of the stones—a marble cross that was being smothered by ivy—and put the light on it. In block letters carved into the base of the cross were the words, OUR BABY MICHAEL—3 DAYS OLD. The one next to it had a simple flat stone on the ground, surrounded by weeds. It read, BABY JESSICA—WITH US ONLY 9 HOURS, WITH GOD FOR ETERNITY. The graves in the old cemetery held babies. A lot of babies.

I did not want to think about it. I broke into a jog and went through the same gap in the fence that Amanda had. I had put the graveyard a few yards behind me when I was finally close enough to see the house.

It was large and tall and looked as dead as the occupants of the small graveyard in front of it. Boards had been nailed over all the windows, like eyes sewn shut, and the old decaying gray house looked ready to collapse under the pressure of a light breeze. I called Amanda a few more times as I got closer to the house, until I stood at the foot of the crooked wooden steps that led up to the covered porch.

Amanda did not respond, but I could hear her laughter in the house, the clump of her low heels on wood.

I went up the steps carefully, opened the creaky door. Aimed the flashlight into the nearly impenetrable darkness inside.

"Amanda?" I called. "I...I'd like to go, if you don't mind."

After a moment of silence, I heard her say something—she had gone upstairs—but not to me. Another garbled voice responded to her. A male voice, deep. Then another, female, broke into raucous, throaty laughter.

*"Amanda*!" I shouted angrily, but I was more nervous than angry. I stepped into the house. The floor was dirty, gritty, and crunched beneath my feet as I went through what was once probably a beautiful foyer. The damp air smelled of mold and... something else. Something like sour body odor.

My flashlight beam passed over sheet-covered furniture hunkering in the dark. A black, dead fireplace with a huge framed painting of some kind on the wall above it, the picture obscured by thick layers of cobwebs and dust as dense and heavy as the sheets on the furniture.

Footsteps sounded overhead. I turned the light upward to the ceiling, held it for a moment on an old chandelier that appeared to be made of cobwebs. I recognized the sound of Amanda's shoes, but there was another set of footsteps that was quieter. Bare feet. Then another, heavier footstep—a single footstep—followed by the whisper of something being dragged. *Thump*—ssshhh... *thump*—ssshhh... *thump*—ssshhh. More voices, pleasant chatter, a girlish laugh.

There was a sound to my right, not far away. I swept the flashlight in the direction of the sound until the beam found an archway that led to another room, and more darkness. It was a shuffling sound accompanied by rapid thumping. I took a couple of steps closer and sent the flashlight beam through the archway. It was a short hall that led to another large room. I saw the corner of a table. Possibly a dining room. I heard the sound again, and the flashlight beam landed on a pair of bare feet. The owner of the feet was on his or her knees and leaning forward. Crawling on the floor, it seemed. But all I could see were the feet. The person in the next room made a sound then, a gurgling, giggling sound, and a quiet, almost whispered stream of nonsense, baby-talk. The voice, like the feet, belonged to a large adult.

Gooseflesh crawled beneath my soaked clothes and my heart pounded in my ears as I turned and rushed back to the front door. But I did not go through it. I still needed the keys to my car.

Then it occurred to me that Amanda was naked. She had nowhere to put the keys, and she had not been carrying them in her hand. So, she had left them in the car.

"Amanda!" I shouted. "I'm leaving! If you want a ride, come *now*!"

I could not get out of that house fast enough, did not even bother to pull the door closed behind me. One of the wooden steps cracked beneath me, but did not break.

When I reached a corner of the cemetery, I heard Amanda's running footsteps slopping through the mud behind me. She giggled as she passed me, ran ahead.

"Party pooper!" she shouted.

I ran to catch up, to get to the car before Amanda and get my keys. But just before I reached it, she opened the driver's side door, ducked into the car, then stood and held up the keys, made them jingle, laughed.

"If you want 'em," she said, grinning, "you're gonna have to *take* 'em from me."

I lunged at her and swiped at the keys, but she jerked them out of my reach, hopped into the car and slammed the door. I suddenly felt as if my feet were made of lead as I went around the car. I did not want to get in, did not want to talk to her.

What had happened back in that little graveyard? What had she done to me?

What was it that had slid wetly between my shoulder blades? I knew what I *thought* it had been, but it made no sense because it was physically impossible for her to have licked my back from her position. How had she squeezed my erection the way she had, when both hands were on my shoulders? How had she touched me down there? And with what?

Amanda started the engine and I got into the car. She made a U-turn and drove away from the graveyard.

"Look, I'd really like to call it a night, okay?" I said. "So, if you don't mind, just drive to wherever you're going and I'll drop you off, then I can go home. Okay?"

"Okay." When she came to the narrow, curvy road that had brought us to the graveyard, she turned right without stopping instead of going back in the direction we had come. She drove in silence for a while, didn't even turn the radio back on. We were going farther up the mountain.

I had never been so uncomfortable in my own car. I kept my eyes front, wondering if, perhaps, I was losing my mind, going a little crazy. At a fork in the road, Amanda went to the right, up a steep incline. I realized I didn't have my seatbelt on and quickly fastened it.

"It's not far," she said. "But you'll have to come in. I want you to meet the folks."

"No, I don't think so."

"Oh, *I* think so," she said with a chuckle.

I ignored the remark. "Who were you talking to? Back there? In the house?"

"What makes you think I was talking to anyone? Maybe I was talking to myself."

"But I heard—there were other—I saw someone *crawling* in the—" I took a deep breath and it trembled as it came out. I tried to still the chaos inside my head and organize my thoughts. "Who does the house belong to?"

"All the houses around here belong to my family."

"So those were relatives?"

She clicked the radio on, turned Joan Jett up loud as she drove through a large, open wrought-iron gate.

And there it was, right in front of me. The house that climbed this side of the mountain. It was not quite as spectacular up close as it was from a distance because I could only see the front rather than the entire, sprawling structure. But looking at it, I could sense its massive size. Had I not known how big the house was, I would have been able to feel it, even sitting there in my car.

Amanda slowed down as she went around the circular driveway and stopped in front of the house. In the center of the circle was a pond and fountain being smothered by ivy. Two black gargoyles sat back to back, wings spread, heads raised, fanged snouts open wide. No water came from their mouths. The fountain looked like it had not been in use for decades.

Amanda turned off the engine, the headlights. "All right, let's go, Andy. You really *must* come meet the folks. Especially my little brother Dexter. I think he'll like you a lot, and he doesn't have *any* friends, so it would do him good to—"

"I'm sorry, but I'd rather just go home."

"Oh. Okay." She opened the door and got out.

"Um, you're still naked," I said.

She leaned back into the car, grinning, her soaked hair flat against her skull, and got her dress, mask, and clutch from the back seat as she said, "Oh, Andy, you have *such* a delicious grasp of the obvious." She slammed the door and hurried toward the house.

With my keys.

"Dammit!" I shouted as I got out of the car, flashlight still in hand. "Hey, you've still got my—"

Amanda interrupted me in a sing-song cadence: "If you *want* 'em, you're gonna have to come *get* 'em!" She hurried up the enormous bell-shaped marble stairs that led to the dark, wooden double doors of the house, each with a large knocker in the center.

A dim light shone high over the doors and cast Amanda's broadening shadow, long and black, down the stairs behind her.

I slammed the car door and ran after her, hoping to reach her before she went into the house. I did not want to have to go inside. The house engulfed my field of vision as I ran toward it, went up the steps two at a time. Almost as if it were lunging at me menacingly, trying to chase me away from a place where I did not belong.

Amanda opened the door and went inside before I reached the top of the stairs.

Beyond the open door, I could see only darkness, and Amanda's shape, a shadow within shadows, turning back to me to say, "Come on, darling, come in out of the rain," as she held her right arm out straight and jangled my ring of keys from one finger. Then she turned and disappeared into the house.

I stopped outside the open door and called, "Aman—Miss

Bollinger, please, I'd like to go home now. Could you…could I have my…" I gave up. My voice seemed to wither and die just inside the house. No one was listening, no one could hear. I had no choice.

With my heart mimicking the sound of the distant thunder, I went inside the Bollinger house.

# Six

The foyer was dark, but there was dim light beyond. I neglected to turn off the flashlight as I entered the front room of the house, and I stood there looking around for a while before I realized it was still shining and clicked it off.

The large room seemed to have been cut out of marble. At one time, it probably had been beautiful, all white with swirls of bluish-gray here and there. A reflection of the fire in the enormous fireplace probably once shimmered on the smooth marble floor.

The shelves probably once held rows of books, maybe beautiful, valuable knick-knacks and trinkets. The large rug on the floor was the color of rust, but looked like it used to be a bright red and blue, or perhaps green. But that was a long time ago. Now, in the dim light from bowl-like wall sconces of filthy frosted glass that glowed upward, the room was alive with dust. The walls were a sickly yellowish-gray. The fireplace was a black cave with old ashes piled high in its yawning mouth. Instead of books, the shelves held what appeared to be nothing more than a collection of junk that made no sense: an old toy dump truck, a rock the size of a baseball still clumped with old, long-dried mud, an ancient colander, a fat black dildo rippled with thick veins, the skeleton of a rodent, an old torn boxing glove, a ceramic poodle with the head missing, a child's birthday card standing open, a small human skull (I did not get close enough to see if it was real or not because I thought it might be), a filthy rusted vice, what appeared to be a real but stuffed iguana, and other equally strange objects, all of them bearing a skin of dust. On the floor along the walls and around the dark wood sofa that faced the fireplace, dust had gathered in large greasy clumps. Grandma called them dust-bunnies. I had never seen them in such great quantity, and something about them made my skin crawl.

The house had a smell similar to the old boarded-up house I had been in earlier.

Stale and moldy, with the odor of unwashed bodies.

There were sounds in the house, but they were not house sounds. Muffled by walls and floors, I could hear constant movement, resonant voices, laughter. Almost like a bus station, or an old hospital busy with activity. The sounds seemed to be coming from all directions at once, but I finally realized they came from above me, upstairs.

Against a far wall, a staircase curved up to the second of four floors. A track ran along the wall beside the stairs. I had seen one like it in a movie once. A chair ran up and down the stairs along the track for someone who was unable to walk. The chair itself was on one of the other floors, or perhaps it had been removed.

A portrait hung on the wall above the fireplace and the figure at its center bled through the layer of dust on the painting. It was a man sitting in a large throne-like chair.

I had trouble making sense of the portrait, so I turned the flashlight back on and aimed the beam at the man in the painting.

"That's my great, great grandfather," Amanda said, and I jumped, startled by her voice. She laughed at me. "You just don't know how to relax, do you?" She had removed her muddy shoes, and was still naked except for her mud-speckled stockings and black garters.

She had a beautiful body, but I was too distracted and nervous, too anxious to leave to pay it any attention. Even if I weren't, I no longer had any desire to touch her body. Or even get very close to it.

"Are you hungry?" Amanda asked. "Would you like something to drink?"

"I'd like my car keys, please."

She laughed. "I guess I put them down somewhere. I'll have to look for them."

She turned and walked away.

Before following her, I turned the flashlight onto the painting again. The man in the portrait had no arms or legs. I turned off the flashlight and followed Amanda.

We ended up in the kitchen. It was spacious, well -lit, with lots of pale tiles and red brick. But it looked as if there had been an earthquake. Nearly every inch of counter-space was cluttered with dishes and glasses, coffee mugs and tea cups, bowls and utensils, pots and pans, all unwashed, stained, crusted with old food. Something was piled in the left side of the two-basin, stainless-steel sink. From where I stood, I could see only the top of the pile, a rounded hump of something wet and black with streaks of green. When I realized it was only a pile of rotting lettuce, or perhaps cabbage, I was so relieved that I failed to be offended by the disgusting sight.

"How about a nice ham and cheese sandwich?" she asked.

"No, thank you."

"Coffee? I'll start a pot right now."

I thought of drinking out of a cup from that kitchen and wondered what I might find at the bottom when I was finished. "No. No coffee, thanks. Just...my keys."

She frowned, looked concerned. Came over to me and raised a hand to place it on my cheek. I almost tripped over my own feet trying to keep away from it, trying to avoid her touch.

Amanda appeared genuinely hurt. "What's wrong, Andy?"

I wanted to shout, *You licked my back while I was on top of you, and you want to know what's wrong? Something that's not* supposed *to be between your legs grabbed my balls, and you want to know what's wrong?*

Instead, I tried to keep my quiet voice steady as I said, "I just want my keys. Please give them to me."

Amanda stepped toward me again, saying, "Oh, please, Andy, won't you—" She stopped for a moment when I backed away from her quickly. Her smile fell away and she dropped her arms loosely at her sides beneath drooping shoulders. "I want you to meet Daddy and the others. At least Dexter, you have to meet Dexter. He's my little brother."

"Maybe...some other time." I knew I would never be

returning to that house, or even to that side of the mountain, ever. But I was trying to be polite and get my keys.

Amanda sighed as she turned and went to a coffee maker on a corner of the messy counter. She took the pot to the sink, where she ignored the pile of ooze. As she filled the pot with water, she said, "Well, I'm sorry, Andy, but it won't be some other time, it's going to be *tonight*. So you might as well have a nice hot cup of coffee, because you're not going anywhere until you meet Daddy. That's why you're here."

"What?"

She went back to the coffee maker, opened the top, and emptied the pot into it. "I didn't stutter."

"What do you mean, that's why I'm here?"

Working around the mess as if it were not there, Amanda did not respond until the coffee was brewing. When she turned to me, I was surprised by her face. The smirking cockiness was gone and she looked sad, vulnerable.

"I thought you liked me," she said.

I did not know what to say.

"Didn't you have *any* fun tonight? *I* had a good time. Even though we didn't...finish." Half her mouth turned up in a smile. But when I did not respond, it went away. She turned her back to me and stared at the gurgling coffee maker as she said, "You think I'm a freak." Her voice sounded thick, as if she were about to cry. I couldn't have that.

"That's funny," I said, trying to sound light. "I didn't think I'd ever hear anyone say that to *me*. It's usually the other way around."

She said nothing.

"Look, I...I don't think you're a freak, Miss Bol—Amanda. That never even crossed my mind," I lied. "You're...you're beautiful. But what happened in the graveyard earlier...the things you did to me...Well, you scared me. Um, a lot. I mean, that's the kind of thing you should warn a guy about, you know? What... whatever it was."

She bowed her head and looked, for a moment, like she was praying to the coffee maker. "I didn't mean to scare you."

"No, of course you didn't." I could not believe what I was

saying, what I was talking about so casually. The woman's tongue had gone down the back of my shirt, and something between her legs had moved and squeezed between mine, and yet we sounded like we were talking about her puppy pissing on my carpet.

Amanda turned to me again, took a few steps toward me but kept a distance.

"Just stick around for a little while longer. I think Daddy's upstairs, he should be down any minute."

My heart would not slow down. Telling a lie did not make it any better, because I have always been a terrible liar. "I'll make you a deal," I said. "Give me my keys, and I'll have a cup of coffee with you and wait for your dad to come down." I smiled, tried to look relaxed. "Okay?"

She studied my face, frowning. "Well…if Daddy found out—" She dropped her voice to a whisper. "—he'd be pretty upset."

I shrugged. "I'm not gonna tell him."

"You promise to stay?"

I smiled. "Sure. I mean, I've seen this house a million times from the road. I've always wondered what it was like inside."

When Amanda came toward me, I resisted the urge to turn and rush out of the kitchen. She moved close, until her body was just an inch or so from mine, put a hand on my shoulder. "I'm one of the people who live here. What do you think of me?"

*Just enough to get the keys,* I told myself as I rested my hand on her hip. Her skin was cool, still slightly damp from the rain. "I think you're beautiful," I said through my forced smile.

"Mmm, that's better. That's *much* better."

She kissed me. I responded, but kept my lips together, even when the tip of her tongue—

*It went down my back! Between my shoulder blades!*

—pressed against them. When she pulled back, frowning, I said, "I'm sorry, but…what if your dad comes in?"

Her face relaxed. "Yeah. You're right. He'd probably get jealous."

*Jealous?* I thought with a frown. "How about my keys? And a cup of coffee?"

"All right. Have a seat." She gestured toward an oval table of dark, scuffed-up wood in front of a large antique hutch that stood against a wall. The hutch was filled with a few ancient-looking plates and cups, and more junk like the odd items on the shelves in the other room. The table was piled high with old yellowed newspapers and magazines and old phone books. "Just push some of that stuff out of your way and clear a space."

I went to one of the six chairs at the table, pulled it away and turned it so I could watch her. Sat down and set my flashlight upright on the floor, pushed some of the newspapers and magazines back with an elbow to make room for my coffee.

Amanda went back to the counter, where the coffee pot was almost full. She pulled open the drawer beneath it, removed my keys and held them up so I could see them. I smiled again. She put the keys on the counter and opened the cupboard overhead. It was empty. She searched the stacks of old dishes and pots and pans until she found two coffee mugs, went to the sink and washed and dried them.

I tried to make small talk. "How old is your little brother?"

"Thirty-eight."

I blinked with surprise. "Thirty-eight? But…how old are you?"

"It's impolite to ask a lady her age."

"Oh, I-I…I'm sorry, I was just—"

She laughed. "I'm kidding, silly! You *know* I'm not a lady. I'm thirty-one."

"But…you just said he's thirty-eight. That makes him older than you."

"Mm-hm. But he's still my little brother." She went back to the counter with the mugs. "How do you like your coffee?" she asked.

"Black is fine."

"A man who takes his coffee black," she said as she poured. "I like that."

With the pinky finger of her left hand hooked through my key ring, she came to the table holding each mug by its handle. I watched the keys on her left hand as she set a mug before me with her right. It was chipped on the bottom edge and on the side it read, Don't talk to me until I've finished my coffee! She put the other mug into her right hand and I reached out for the keys.

Amanda dropped them into my coffee and giggled. She went to a chair across from me and sat down, put her coffee on the table. "Now you'll just *have* to sit there and drink your coffee first."

I clenched my teeth angrily and dipped my fingers in the coffee, scooped the keys off the bottom of the mug. It was very hot, and as I pulled my hand out, I stood so suddenly, I knocked the chair over. "Son of a *bitch*," I muttered to myself, shaking my hand, wiping my burned fingers on my cold wet jeans. I leaned down and grabbed my flashlight.

"What are you doing?" she asked, surprised, confused. "You said you would—"

"I lied," I said as I turned to leave the kitchen, slipping the keys into my pocket.

A wheelchair zipped through the doorway with an electronic hum and headed straight for me. In the chair sat what appeared to be a very small old man with a large head and a deeply creased and rugged face that seemed to hang from the skull.

"Andy Sayers!" he said loudly. He was not shouting, he simply had a very loud, booming, gravelly voice.

My mouth dropped open when I realized he was not small at all. His legs ended where his knees should have begun. He wore a dirty, white sleeveless undershirt and dark green pants that had been cut and sewn shut at the ends of the legs. From each side of his face, skin hung all the way to his round belly—two long, wrinkled, milk-pale jowls that fell over his chest like the scrotum of a great bull.

I bit my lower lip to keep from crying out in horror.

The wheelchair stopped abruptly just a few feet in front of me and the man hopped out, landed with a loud thump on the ends of his leg-stumps. He waddled toward me and held out his left hand to shake. His right arm was not an arm at all. It was the size of a toddler's arm, but twisted, resembling a large plucked turkey wing that came to a dull, flabby point with no hands or fingers. I backed away without realizing what I was doing, but he kept coming. He didn't even notice—or care—that I didn't want him to touch me or get near me. My back bumped against the side of the hutch and he grabbed my left hand with his, huge and knobby and liver-spotted, and shook it.

"I'm Matthew Bollinger," he said, and his voice vibrated through my bones. He dropped my hand, backed up. "But you can call me Matt, hell, ever'body calls me Matt."

Amanda stood and said, "Hello, Daddy."

Bollinger grinned at her and showed small teeth that were spaced apart. He climbed onto the chair I'd been sitting in, got on the table, and waddled unsteadily but aggressively over the newspapers and magazines to Amanda. She put her left arm around him. Her right hand fondled and caressed the wrinkled sacks of flesh that hung from his face as they kissed. For a long time.

I turned to leave, but Bollinger said, "You have fun with m'girl at that party, Andy?"

He did not give me a chance to answer. "We're not the partyin' type in this house, y'know. We're Christians, and Halloween parties don't 'zactly fit into our way a life, 'cause they don't fit into God's plan. But I told her t'go an' bring y'back here 'cause I figgered it was time we met and had ourselves a li'll talk."

The top of his large head was bald, speckled with liver spots. Thin, stringy, yellowed gray hair grew around the sides and in the back. His right ear was about an inch higher than the left, and both were large and gnarled.

"I've been wantin' t'talk to you," he said as he got off the table.

"Muh*me*?" I croaked.

"Yeah, you!" He smiled around all those tiny teeth, laughed, and the flesh hanging from his jaw jiggled and swayed. "Siddown, drink your coffee, don't stand on my 'count."

I went to the chair and slowly lowered myself into it. Set the flashlight across my lap as he returned to his wheelchair, settled in, still smiling.

Amanda returned to her chair, still naked but apparently

comfortable with it, not at all self-conscious.

"Tell me, Andy," Bollinger said. "Why'd you quit? How come?"

My mouth was dry, so I sipped the coffee. "Quit? I…I'm not sure I know what you—"

"College!" he boomed. "How come y'dropped outta college, huh?"

"Well, I…I-I-I…I'm not a religious person," I stammered.

"*What*? I thought your gramma was a good God-fearin' Christian."

A chill went through me. How did he know? "She is, but… I'm not."

Bollinger looked at me with concern, stroked the dangling skin like a beard. "Well, son…what about your soul?"

"My…soul?"

"Yeah! Your eternal soul! Don't you worry 'bout what'll happen to it when you die? Hell, you almost died *once* already in that fire, what about when it *really* happens, huh?" He turned to Amanda. "Cuppa coffee, sugar?"

As he continued, she got up and washed a mug for him, hurried to the coffee pot and poured, took it to him, then returned to her chair.

"The soul's all we got in the end, boy," he said. "Gotta make sure we know where it's goin' when we check out. That's all religion is, really—soul insurance. Take me, for example. I'm a bidnessman. Gotta lotta money, a *whole* lot. Betcha didn't know that."

I nodded slightly. "I've heard."

"I gotta protect all that money, and the things I buy with it. I got so much insurance, it's comin' outta my nose like milk when I laugh too hard." He laughed. "But they don't sell insurance for the soul, boy. Y'can't get a piece a the rock for your eternal soul.

Gotta get that from God. From religion. Y' *do* believe in *God,* don't cha?"

Thanks to the alcohol I had consumed, I was not thinking clearly, so I was hardly in the mood to start mulling over weighty issues like God and my eternal soul. "I…I guess so," I lied.

"Y' *guess*?"

"Yeah, I believe in God."

"Okay, then, here's the deal. When you go back to school, y'listen to what them Bible teachers have to say, y'hear? They's a lot to learn from the Bible. See, I never had no schoolin'. My momma taught me to read with the Bible. Learned a lot. Made me the man I am today. My momma taught me to read it, and my uncle-daddy taught me how t'interpret it."

*Uncle-daddy?* I thought. For a moment, I wondered if I was dreaming and would wake up soon, dripping with sweat in my bed but immensely relieved. But I could still smell the house's odor, and the coffee—I had never smelled anything in a dream before.

"But, um, I don't have any plans to go back," I said. My voice had withered and become very quiet. "I plan to leave the Village soon."

His broad face darkened as his bushy eyebrows huddled together over the bridge of his flat, broken nose. "*Leave*? Where ya goin'?"

"I don't know. Yet."

"Well, don't even think about it no more. You stayin' put." He grinned, but his frown did not go away. "I got plans for you, Andrew Sayers."

They were probably the most terrifying words I had ever heard in my life. I could not speak.

Bollinger sipped his coffee, then put the mug on the corner of the table. "I been watchin' you since you came to the Village."

He seemed to expect me to be happy about that. "Wuh… watching me?"

"Oh, yeah. Hell, I know ever little thing goes on 'round these parts. Nobody comes an' goes 'round here I don't hear about it. When you came…Well, you caught my eye."

"I did?" I swallowed, and it made a clicking sound in my throat.

"Sure ya did. A boy like you?"

I turned to Amanda. She was watching her father, listening closely. When she saw me turn, she smiled at me for a moment. It was a happy, thrilled smile that seemed to say, *Isn't this exciting?*

"When you came here after your, uh, accident," Bollinger continued, "I kept a close eye on you. Sumpin tol' me you was worth watchin'. And I was right. You was smart beyond your years when y'got here, and you got nothin' but smarter."

There was an explosion of activity and sound in the hall outside the kitchen doorway that startled me enough to make me jump in the chair. Three young, shrill voices—two of them shrieking and the third laughing—drew closer, until two children ran into the kitchen, one chasing the other.

"Hey, hey kids!" Amanda called, getting up and going to them, arms outstretched.

"Whoa, quiet down, okay? We're trying to talk in here."

The children stopped running and fell silent as they turned to Amanda.

I watched them for a moment, then reached up and rubbed my eyes hard with a thumb and two fingers. When I looked at the children again, nothing had changed. My eyes were fine.

"Come here, come here," Amanda said, taking their hands. She led them toward us. "We have company. A very special visitor." She smiled at me as she got down on one knee between the children and put an arm around each of them. "Andy, this is my son, Daniel. And these are my nieces, Sharon and Karen, my sister's daughters."

They were just children, and I wanted so much to smile at them as if I were happy to meet them, as if there were nothing at all wrong with them. I wanted to smile at them the way so many people had never smiled at me since I was burned, to make them feel good. To make them feel normal. I think I even tried to smile, stretched the corners of my mouth out and up, and tried to speak, to say hello, to tell them it was nice to meet them. But whatever was on my face, it was not a smile, and the closest I came to speaking was an abrupt choking sound in my throat.

Judging by the way they stared at me and tried to back away—Amanda held them in place—they seldom if ever received visitors. Maybe they found me as shocking as I found them.

"Kids, this is Andy Sayer," Amanda said. "Can you say hello to Andy?"

Both of the girl's heads said, "Hello, Andy."

The boy made a sound that resembled the word "hello." It was difficult to tell how old he was. Maybe eight, maybe ten, maybe even older. His body was bent—possibly a curved spine—and he was slightly hunched. His oversized head was misshapen as well, and his vacant eyes were narrow and slanted. He was naked except for a diaper that hung on him heavily as if it needed changing. After he'd stood in front of me for several seconds, I realized that was the case because I could smell it. His arms were at his sides, and at the end of them, instead of hands, were two curved protrusions of flesh that came to points. Like lobster claws, but of soft, flabby flesh.

The girl wore a nice red dress. She was about ten years old, with a thick body.

The heads were pressed close together and looked uncomfortable. Identical dark brown hair with braided pigtails, identical blue eyes, identical pug noses. Two voices that spoke almost simultaneously.

Amanda laughed. "Well, Andy, aren't you going to say hello?"

Somehow, I pulled myself together. "Hi, kids," I said. "Nice to meet you."

To the children, Amanda said, "Why don't you go give Daddy a kiss, now, okay? Then it's time for bed. In fact, it's *past* your bedtime."

I expected them to leave the kitchen then. Instead, they went to the wheelchair.

Bollinger leaned forward and let them kiss his cheek. Two children, three kisses.

*Daddy?* I thought. I began to tremble then as I wished I were home in bed.

Where I belonged.

"Daniel, go have your aunt Maggie change that diaper," Amanda said.

Bollinger sipped his coffee. "Now, where was I? I was talkin' 'bout your smarts, yeah. You was smart. That was plain as day. After you graduated from Mount Crag High, I figgered you'd go to college. If not here, then somewheres else. When you didn't,

I was a li'll worried, gotta admit. Boy as smart as you needs a good education, some direction and guidance. See, most a my family—we're a big family, the Bollingers, but never been too big on learnin'. We're...differnt. Like you. Differnt, unique. People don't unnerstand us, so we don't mix with 'em much, if y'know what I mean."

I didn't know what he meant. They were not like me. I was "differnt" because of an accident, a fire. I had not been born with my scars.

"Anyways, I decided you needed a good college education," Bollinger continued.

"So I sent you to Hand of God. Bet you din't know that was me." He smiled.

I saw no point in telling him it had crossed my mind, and simply shook my head.

"But then you quit." He frowned again. It made him look dangerous. He took a deep breath and shook his head. "I gotta tell ya, Andy, that din't make me very happy.

"No, sir. You *need* that learnin', boy. You're smart as a whip, but for what I got planned for you, you gotta have some *schoolin'*."

Ice water coursed through my veins and goosebumps rose beneath my wet clothes. Until that moment, I had been scared because of them, because of what they looked like. But Bollinger's words made me realize I was in real trouble, that I had been brought to that massive house on the mountainside for a reason and whatever it was, it wasn't social.

I took another swallow of coffee, then stood, holding the flashlight in my right hand. "Um, I really appreciate the coffee, but I've got to get home and—"

"Now, just hold on a second, boy," Bollinger said, raising his hand. "Sit, sit, just sit back down, you can go when we're done talkin'."

"Daddy, I think he should meet Dexter," Amanda said.

"Sure, honeybuns, he will, soon as we're done talkin'. Whyn't you go on upstairs and check on Dexter, make sure he's ready for comp'ny."

Amanda went to her father's side, leaned down and wrapped her arms around him. She whispered something into his big ear as she ran a hand over his chest and stomach, down to his lap, then back up again, slowly, fingers moving, exploring lovingly.

Whatever she said made Bollinger laugh a deep, rumbling laugh, and then she laughed, too, before leaning down to kiss him again. It was a wet, noisy kiss, and Bollinger reached around to caress, then squeeze, his daughter's shapely bare ass.

The coffee burned inside me as it rose dangerously close to my throat. I looked away and swallowed hard several times.

When Amanda left, I sat in the chair again, but on the very edge, ready to go.

Bollinger rolled his wheelchair close to me, leaned forward and stared at me for several long seconds, smiling.

"I ain't gettin' any younger, Andy," he said quietly. "I'm the head a this family.

"Whatcha cal the *patriarch*. Have been since I was about your age. Next May, I'll be seventy years old. My health ain't so good. I've already lived longer'n my own poppa.

"Hel, longer'n anybody in this family's lived for a long time. Ain't nobody in this family fit to run it. I gotta lotta boys, but they ain't...Well, they just ain't fit to take the reins in their hands, y'know what I mean? That's why I been watchin' you. You know what I said to m'self first time I saw you, Andy? I said to m'self, that boy could be my son." He grinned.

"It's true. You're not like the others out there, all them perfect people who think their shit don't stink. You're one of us, Andy. You could be a Bollinger. An' that's what I wanna make ya. I want you t'be one a the family and take over all my bidness interests when I go." He sat back in his wheelchair looking satisfied with himself, waiting for my response. He expected me to be happy, excited. It was in his face, his small eyes.

I wanted to throw up. "Why...me?" I asked. It came out as an unintentional whisper.

"I *toldja*! 'Cause you're so smart! Hell, you could prob'ly do it without any college learnin', but I think it'd do you good to finish your education. Sharpen you up, make a good Christian outta ya. We're a Christian family, the Bollingers, and we don't take to no godless people sharin' a roof with us, know what I mean?"

I considered shooting out of the chair and running by him, getting out of the house. But I did not trust my knees, my legs. I was trembling all over and felt like melting butter.

I said, "But I, uh, I really don't want to...look, um, there are plenty of smart people who could—"

"Not like you, there ain't. Like I said, Andy, you're one of us."

I closed my eyes and shook my head, which was beginning to throb. Too much alcohol, too much...Bollinger. "I don't know what you mean when you say I'm one of you, what...what does that mean?"

"I gotta spell it out for ya, boy?"

Someone entered the kitchen quietly. A pregnant woman in a housedress, plain and powder-blue, with old faded-yellow stains on the skirt. Her round belly looked ready to explode, and her small head was bald and slanted sharply backward from the pronounced ridge of her brow to a dull, rounded point on top. People like her used to work in carnival freak shows and were called "pinheads." Doctors called them microcephalics.

She was short, just under five feet, with a flat, broad nose and large rubbery lips. No teeth. Her dull eyes swam in her head with the eternal happiness of the feeble-minded as she stepped up behind Bollinger, reached around and playfully put her large masculine hands, with half-moons of dark green grime beneath the edges of her fingernails, over his eyes.

Bollinger smiled. "Okay, now, lessee...who's this? Is it... could it be...Daisy?"

The woman's small head bobbed up and down as she guffawed like a cartoon character. She stepped around the wheelchair and stroked the top of Bollinger's head gently, lovingly, still laughing.

He put his arm around her, his hand on her flat, broad behind, which appeared to be bare beneath the dress, and said, "Andy, I'd like you t'meet my daughter Daisy." He looked up at her, raised his voice a little. "Daisy, this is my friend Andy Sayer, from the Village."

Daisy stepped toward me and curtsied clumsily. She spoke, but it was incomprehensible, thick-tongued babble. The body-odor smell of the house was very strong around Daisy, and I made an effort not to curl my nose and wince.

"She don't talk so good," Bollinger said, "but that don't stop 'er from talkin'. Ain't that right, Daisy?"

She turned and faced him, guffawing again. Daisy got down on her knees and started to unbutton his pants.

Bollinger pushed her away gently. "No, no, Daisy, honey, not now. I got some jawin' to do with Andy, okay?"

She stood and patted Bollinger's bald head, then went to the doorway. Before leaving, she turned to me and waved a big hand. Babbled something that was vaguely understandable: "Bye-bye, Andy. Bye-bye."

Bollinger took the coffee mug from the table and gulped the rest of it down. Put it back on the table and smiled at me, moving a toggle-switch on the arm of his wheelchair. It backed away with a mechanical whir.

"Let's go on upstairs," he said. "You can meet Dexter an' some a the others.

"They'll be happy to see ya, prob'ly. We don't get many visitors here."

As I followed Bollinger to the stairs, I looked for the right moment to bolt. It never came, because there were always others in my path. Others I was afraid would reach out and grab me as I passed.

Outside the kitchen, we encountered two large men joined at the hip, wearing only a single enormous robe tied at the waist. Bollinger introduced them as his nephews, Charles and Rodney.

A young man with no legs and fleshy flippers where he should have had arms, crawled over the floor. Another of Bollinger's nephews, Benny.

Bollinger's wife, Wanda, met us on the stairs as I walked up next to the electronic chair that carried Bollinger slowly along its track. She clutched the bannister with her right hand as she made her way slowly down the stairs wearing an orange pantsuit that looked like it might have been in style in the early seventies. In her left hand, she carried a cane, which she held out ahead of her, touching each stair with it before she stepped down. Wanda's eye sockets were empty. The skin that grew over them was sunken deeply beneath her brow, forming two pools of shadow. Bollinger asked her what Dexter was up to and she said he'd just had a snack. As she passed, I caught a glimpse of the thick, pink, fleshy tail that tapered to the floor from a slit in her pantsuit. She was Bollinger's wife, but I wondered in what other way they were related.

"You're one of us, Andy," Bollinger said, "because you're differnt. Know what I mean? Maybe not in the same way, but still differnt. People stare, don't they? They're suspicious of you, like your burned face makes you some kinda bad person, huh? A monster? I bet kids're scared of you, too. And when *you* were a kid, I bet they picked on you, didn't they? Huh?"

I didn't reply.

"Sure they did. Most people get that kinda treatment, it scars 'em. And I don't mean physically. Makes 'em bitter, mean. Not you, though. You're polite, friendly. You say you ain't a Christian, but I'll tell ya sumpin, they's a lotta Christians could take a lesson from you. You behave the way our lord an' savior Jesus Christ wants us *all* to behave. Wish I could say the same, boy. Now me…'fraid I got m'self a mean streak." He laughed as we reached the third floor. He got out of the chair on the track and climbed into a waiting wheelchair. "But the rest of my family, they couldn't be sweeter. You won't get none of that starin' and meanness from them like you do from the people out there," he said, nodding vaguely toward a wall, indicating the outside. "They'd take y'in like you's one of the family. Hell, far as I'm concerned, y'already are. My family's your family,

Andy," he said, smiling up at me. "And when I'm gone, it's *all* yours. Everything."

As I climbed the stairs, the smell had gotten stronger, closer. The voices and activity from upstairs had grown louder. With each step, my feet grew heavier, my heart pounded harder, faster. I barely heard what Bollinger was saying—I was too busy trying to decide what to do next. But oddly enough, I found myself not wanting to offend him.

As revolted as I was by everything and everyone I had seen—except the children, who broke my heart, the poor, innocent children—Bollinger had been nothing but pleasant.

Otherwise, it would have been much easier.

I said, "I…I'm sorry, Mr. Bollinger, but I'm—"

*"Matt!"* he thundered. "Cal me Matt. No formalities here, boy."

I walked slowly down the hall beside his wheelchair. It was a long hallway, and at the end, I could see that another hallway formed a T-shaped intersection. There were doors on each side, nothing but doors. No paintings or photographs on the gray walls, no plants, nothing decorative. Just doors, most of them open, people going in and out of the rooms, crossing the hall to enter other rooms. Some walking upright, some hunched, others crawling. The smell was powerful, and I could no longer hide my revulsion.

"I can't help you, Matt," I said without looking at him.

"Oh? How come?" I heard a smirk in his voice.

"I've got other plans."

"And what plans'd they be?"

"Plans. For my life. I…I'm going to be leaving the Village tomorrow. And I won't be coming back." That had not been my plan, of course. Not until that very moment.

The wheelchair's whir reached a higher pitch as Bollinger sped ahead, then spun the chair around to face me. I stumbled to a stop. He was smiling.

"You ain't got no plans to leave, son," he said. His voice was low and still pleasant, but with a new edge I had not heard before. "If you did, I'd know sumpin about it. Like I said, Andy, nothin' happens on this mountain I don't know about. And I been watchin' you special. You're just…nervous, assall. You gotta letcherself get used to the idea. You'll get more love an' acceptance here'n you ever got in your whole life, Andy.

"And remember…I'm rich. Real rich. *You'll* be rich, too."

Up ahead, Amanda leaned out of an open door, still naked.

"What's taking you two so long?" she asked with a laugh.

"Let's go," Bollinger said. "Once you meet Dexter, I'll give you a tour a the place so you can get to know your way around."

I started to tell him I wasn't staying, but knew it would do no good. The man had made up his mind. There just didn't seem to be a whole lot of his mind left. I was convinced he was no different than anyone else I had met in the house, mentally deficient in some way.

"Now, when ya meet Dex," he said as we continued down the hall, "don't let 'im put y'off. He's a little, uh...what's the word? Hyper. Know what I mean? He's one a them kids just can't hold still. Might take you a while t'get used to 'im, but just remember, he only wants to play, assall."

"I thought Amanda said he was thirty-eight."

"Yeah, but still, he's just a kid," he said with a chuckle.

Bollinger went ahead of me, turned right and went through the door Amanda had leaned out of a moment earlier.

The room was dimly lit by a small lamp on a table in the corner, and the smell was stronger in there than it had been anywhere else in the house. There were three chairs in the room, and colorful, childish drawings were tacked to the walls. A small rectangular window looked out at the night.

Amanda sat in one of the chairs beside what appeared to be a baby's bassinet.

She was leaning forward, smiling, talking quietly. I could see movement inside the small bed. I stopped just inside the door as Bollinger wheeled over to the bassinet.

"Hey, Dex!" Bollinger said with a grin. "Gotta visitor. Andy here's the one I been tell in' y'about. From the Village." He peered over the edge of the bassinet. "How ya doin', huh, boy? I ain't seen ya all day, I been on the phone, on the computer. Whatcha been up to?"

The sound that came from the bassinet went through my head like a bullet. It was the squeal of a pig and the cry of a child, and it knocked the breath from my lungs.

Bollinger laughed, then said, "Whatcha got there, Dex?"

From the bassinet came a gurgling response.

"You still playin' with *that* thing? Here, gimme that." Bollinger grabbed something, pulled it up out of the bassinet. It was a woman's purse, dark blue leather, a long shoulder strap. It looked familiar. "C'mon, now, leggo," Bollinger said. There was no longer any laughter in his voice. He sounded frustrated as he pulled on the purse, raised his voice. "I *toldja* y'couldn't play with that no more, Dex! We gonna hafta get rid of it!"

Just above the edge of the bassinet, I could see a hand gripping the purse's shoulder strap. No, that's not the right word—it wasn't a hand. But it was at the end of a fat, squat arm, where a hand should have been, with skin the color of buttermilk. There were only two fat fingers and something that resembled a thumb. An inverted triangle of digits. Growing from the end of each was something that nature had intended to be a fingernail. Translucent, thick, and curved to a sharp point. The claws were hooked into the leather strap and pulled stubbornly.

Soft light glinted off of something on the front of the purse, something silver. Two letters on the purse's flap, initials: CF.

Carla Firth.

I thought of her casket being lowered into the ground that morning, of the brief but upsetting description of the remains of her corpse in the newspaper, found in a small clearing on Mt. Crag. Torn, broken. I remembered what Carrie had overheard in the diner between Chief Ledbetter and the retired forensics expert from the city—

*Whoever did that to Carla Firth? It wasn't a who. This guy says it couldn't be human, that it's an animal, most likely a bear. And he thinks the same thing happened to the others. The ones he reviewed, anyway.*

—and I imagined those deadly, malformed fingernails slicing easily through Carla's soft flesh.

Amanda rushed to my side smiling, hooked her arm through mine and said,

"Come meet my little brother," as she pulled me toward the bassinet.

I resisted, but she pulled harder.

*"No!"* I shouted, jerking my arm away from her. I backed toward the door.

Bollinger looked at me with a dark expression. "There's no call t'act like that,

Andy."

"I have to go," I said, my voice broken. "It's late. My grandma will worry."

"Your gramma knows where y'are," Bollinger said with a

nod. "They's nothin' to worry about."

I suddenly felt light-headed, as if my head were floating away from my body like a balloon. "What? What…what do you mean, she knows where I am?"

"I've talked to 'er. We worked ever'thing out. Y'know, she's been worried 'bout you ever since you quit school. She's glad I'll be takin' you in, givin' you a purpose, some good Christian learnin'."

"D-did…did she know…that you were the one…who paid my tuition?"

"Course she knew. Your gramma's a good woman, she wouldn't take nothin' like that from a stranger, outta the blue." He held out his hand, waggled his four fingers, beckoning me with a smile. "Now, c'mon over here and meet Dexter."

Although I was still afraid and disgusted, anger swelled inside me. "I'm leaving," I said flatly, my teeth tightly clenched. I turned to go.

The two large, beefy conjoined twins, Charles and Rodney, filled the open doorway. They stared at me with four dumb eyes. As they turned slightly sideways and stepped into the room, I backed away from them.

Sound and movement exploded behind me, and I spun around. The thing in the bassinet had launched itself through the air with a gut-shriveling squeal, naked, trailing a fat, stubby tail. It landed on the floor with a harsh clicking of claws, and immediately jumped forward again, using its powerful tail to push away from the floor. It was a blur of yellowish white as it bounded toward me and landed just a couple of feet in front of me.

The only part of the creature I saw clearly, the part that made me scream as if something in my mind had snapped, was the large vertical mouth that split open its fat, moist face like a wound beneath a tiny, flat nose, all in the shadow of its bulbous cranium. And teeth, a lot of teeth in the black-and-pink mottled gums.

I spun around and swung the flashlight blindly, high and hard. It connected with the side of Rodney's head, and he and Charles fell like a tree. Next thing I knew, I was running as fast as I could down the long, smelly, noisy hall. It was even noisier than before, and I realized that was because I was still screaming.

I heard the whir of Bollinger's wheelchair behind me as he shouted, "Stop him! Somebody stop him!"

And something else, something closer. The slap of bare feet and the click of claws on the floor, and wet, gurgling breathing, closing the gap between us.

# Seven

"Where y'think you're goin', boy!" Bollinger shouted, and his voice filled the hall way. "No matter where you go, you *gonna* hafta come back here! Y'hear me?" He shouted even louder and I could feel his voice in the floor beneath my feet. *"You don't know it yet, boy, but you gonna hafta come back here 'cause you got nowheres else t'go!"*

His words meant nothing to me. The stairs were just ahead, but before I got there, Daisy appeared, accompanied by a middle-aged man walking on his hands. His body ended at the waist, and he used his thick arms as legs, hands flat on the floor.

When Daisy saw me running, she clapped her big hands and jumped up and down happily.

I slammed between Daisy and her companion and headed down the stairs as Dexter released a long, piercing shriek.

On the second floor landing, I jumped over an armless, legless person—I could not tell if it was male or female—moving slowly over the floor with a rhythmic rocking motion, a string clenched between its teeth. At the end of the string, it dragged a yellow toy duck on wheels that made a squeaking sound as it rolled.

Dexter's feet and claws slapped and clicked on the steps behind me, moving fast.

It was at the bottom of the stairs that I made my mistake and lost my bearings.

Too frightened and frantic to realize it, I turned in the wrong direction and ran for the back of the house rather than the front.

A woman holding a naked, flippered baby stepped out of a doorway and turned to me. In the center of her face was a dark, wet hole, vaguely shaped like the number 8, with the bottom larger than the top. The hole started at her lower lip and ended just beneath her eyes. Mucous glistened around the edges and her twitching tongue was plainly visible in her mouth. I tried to go around her, but my shoulder slammed into hers and knocked her against the wall. I heard her moist gasp as I passed, and she shouted something behind me. It was nothing more than sad-sounding nasal honks.

Farther back, Dexter made his pig-like squeal again. He was getting closer.

I rounded a corner, ducked through a narrow archway, and found myself in a small room with a lamp glowing in the corner. Two people were seated on a sofa watching television. I did not look at them, did not want to see them.

There was no way out of the room except the archway through which I'd come.

But there were pale yellow curtains drawn over a window. As the two people on the sofa stood and hurried out, frightened, I tore the curtains open. A large rectangular window looked out on the night. Without hesitation, I grabbed a wooden straight back chair against the wall, held it by its back, and swung it in an arc at the window. The shattering sound was deafening and a scream rose from just outside the room. With two more quick sweeps of the chair, I knocked the large, jagged shards of glass that pointed upward like transparent fangs from the frame. Tossed the chair aside and threw myself into the darkness outside.

To my left, the house continued up the side of the mountain like a giant, curved, meandering staircase. Filled with people conceived in ways no one was meant to be conceived, bearing the hideous marks of their genetics.

I heard wet snorting behind me, another squeal. Running blindly in the rainy dark, I clicked on the flashlight, and the beam sparkled through the heavily pouring rain. It fell on a black pond not three feet in front of me. Raindrops danced on its glossy, lumpy surface between groups of lily pads growing thick in the water. I tried to turn, but my feet slipped through the thick, loose mud and I went in.

After the splash, there was a moment of pleasant, throbbing silence. Trouble-free and safe. When my head broke the surface and I stood in the water—it came halfway up my abdomen and smelled and tasted foul—I heard Dexter's ragged cry and turned.

He had launched himself into the air again and was headed straight for me, a pale, fleshy, screaming missile. I backed up in the water as quickly as I could, rising out of the pond as the bottom slanted sharply upward on the side opposite where I had fallen in. But I was not fast enough. Dexter hit me hard in the chest and knocked me backward into the water. My instinct was to gasp for breath because the impact had emptied my lungs, but I could not get my face above water.

Dexter's hands closed on my shoulders with amazing strength and his claws pierced my shirt. I heard my own panicked voice in my head as it bubbled out of my mouth in the black water. My hands tangled in the lily pads as I struggled. The instant Dexter fell off me, I lifted my head out of the water. I coughed, sucked air deep into my lungs, then coughed some more as I got to my feet and climbed up and out of the pond.

Dexter was near the edge, waist-deep in the pond. His up-and-down mouth yawned open as he released a hitching, throaty wail. He clapped his clawed, mutated hands together and jumped up and down on his tail in the water.

He lunged out of the water, straight for me, arms outstretched, still making that high-pitched staccato sound—

*...he only wants to play, assall.*

—mouth open wide, all those teeth gleaming wetly.

Holding it by the still-lit end with both hands, I swung the flashlight like a baseball bat as Dexter closed in, filling my field of vision. It struck his large, overhanging forehead with a horrible crack, and the light fluttered as Dexter tumbled backward into the water. If any damage had been done, it was only to my Mag-Lite. My hands ached from the impact with Dexter's large round forehead. It was like striking a boulder.

I turned around and tried to run up the slope on this side of the pond. Like a comically frightened character in a Scooby-Doo cartoon, I ran in place for a moment, my feet sliding through the mud.

Dexter splashed in the pond behind me. Once I gained some traction and started putting distance between us, he let out a ululating bawl.

From the corner of my eye, I could see Bollinger sitting in his wheelchair on the other side of the broken window, watching me. A black, hunkering silhouette against the room's pale light.

Running through the dark, the flashlight's flickering beam danced ahead of me, bobbing and sweeping. Although it trembled weakly, the beam kept me from slamming into a fence with a crooked gate. As I fumbled with its rusted metal latch, Dexter's bare feet slapped in the mud behind me. Closer, closer, unfazed by the blow I had landed with the Mag-Lite.

I threw the latch and pulled the gate open, tried to pull it closed behind me. On the other side, a gravel path ran along an outer wall of the house. I kicked up small rocks behind me as I ran. As wet as I was, I should have been cold, but I felt nothing.

My body was numb, and my mind was focused on only one thing: getting to my car.

With gravel crunching under his feet behind me, Dexter repeated a series of grunting, gurgling sounds. I tried to ignore them as I rounded the front corner of the house, jumped over some low shrubs. But they were more than just sounds. It almost sounded as if he were trying to speak. Perhaps he was, but I could not understand him and was not interested.

The Beetle was in sight, still parked in the circular drive between the front steps and the dead gargoyle fountain. I ran faster as Dexter's footsteps grew closer. I wondered if that was the last sound Carla had heard before her death: Dexter closing in behind her.

As I neared the car, I hoped I had not locked the door. It was another habit Grandma had ingrained in me. I put the flashlight in my left hand and wriggled the fingers of my right into the soaking wet pocket of my jeans. Hooked one finger in the key ring and pulled it out.

I hurried around the rear of the car, grabbed the handle. The door opened. I threw the flashlight in ahead of me, slammed the door and locked it with my elbow as I stabbed the key at the ignition. It missed the first time, the second.

The entire car rocked as Dexter landed on the back and I dropped the keys. His claws scraped over the roof with harsh, shrill squealing sounds.

I leaned around the steering wheel and groped for the keys on the floorboard. My lungs burned and my heart felt ready to explode. My fingers were numb and couldn't even feel the rubber mat under my feet. But I heard the keys jingle. Closed my hand on them, sat up, and screamed.

Dexter was lying on the roof of the car with his head resting on the windshield, staring at me. Upside-down, he looked even more like something from a nightmare. Tiny eyes on the bottom, horribly wrong mouth on top, drooling in the rain. He slapped his hands onto the glass and slowly closed both into three-digit fists. His pale claws dug into the glass crunchingly and sliced six white trails.

He made those sounds again, muffled now. Slower, with more clarity. Over and over, until I understood what he was saying.

I slid the key into the ignition, turned it. The Beetle sputtered to life.

Dexter did not seem to notice. He continued making those sounds, saying those words.

I put the car in gear and pushed the accelerator to the floor. The Beetle lurched forward.

Dexter did not move.

I slammed my foot on the brake pedal. The car jerked to a stop and Dexter hit the front of the car once before falling off. I put the car in reverse and backed into the shrubs. Shifted, drove forward and around the fountain.

It occurred to me, before backing up, to run over Dexter. But I could not bring myself to do that, because in spite of his age, I kept thinking of him as a child. Hideous and terrifying, but a child. Even as I sped out of the circular driveway, I could hear him behind me, saying those words.

"Come…play…wiff me! Come…play…wiff me! Come…play…wiff me!"

# Eight

I drove faster that night than I had at any time in my life, faster than my poor old Beetle had ever gone, even with Amanda at the wheel. But I wasn't sure where I was, or where I was going. I was so upset and panicky, I had been driving for about five minutes before I gave it any thought, and I realized I had turned the wrong way as I drove through the wrought iron gate of the Bollinger house. I was going up the mountain again.

The road was too narrow to make a U-turn, and I was afraid to leave the road for fear of running into Dexter again, or some other member of the family. It was unlikely that he would be able to keep up with me on foot, but he could cover a lot of ground bounding forward on that tail. I did not want to take any chances and hoped, instead, that the road would somehow get me back on a main road that would take me into town.

I decided the best thing to do was go straight to the police station in Mount Crag and report what I had seen.

The road wound through the forest, apparently aimless in its backtracking and meandering. Going around a curve, the headlights cut between the trunks of the tall pines to fall briefly on another old house nestled in the woods. I wondered if there were any Bollingers living there, shuffling around in the dark upper floors, waiting for company. My foot pressed on the accelerator a little harder.

After about twenty minutes of driving, I began to worry that I had made a terrible mistake, that the road would take me nowhere.

A few minutes after that, the pavement ended abruptly up ahead, and I braked hard. Where the pavement stopped, mud took over and sloped downward slightly. The way tall pines and firs grew all around the end of the road, it was obvious it had never gone any further. It simply stopped.

I sat there a moment with the engine idling. Remembered Amanda driving off the road and into a ditch earlier that night. It had scared the hell out of me, because I thought she had lost control of the car, but she had not. It had been necessary to drive off the main road and through that ditch to get onto the road that led up the mountain to the main Bollinger house, as well as the others that stood dead and gray in the woods.

I wondered if it was necessary to do the same to get off that road.

Taking a deep breath, I drove forward slowly. The trees were spaced apart enough for me to wind around them. On the other side, a broad ditch ran with a roiling stream of water. Beyond that, a familiar two-lane road—Mt. Crag Pass.

I released a long, groaning sigh of relief, but I had not gotten there yet. Hoping the ditch wasn't too deep, I drove forward slowly, cautiously, and picked up a little speed as the Beetle dipped into the ditch. It was shallow, and I put it behind me in seconds, turned right, and hit the accelerator hard.

On the pass and heading over the mountain, I felt safer, but not *safe*. I had no idea how many houses the Bollingers had on the mountain, or how many Bollingers there were. For all I knew, they were coming after me in cars, making their way through the woods to cut me off up ahead. I glanced nervously at the rearview mirror as I drove, tense and jumpy.

As I passed the sign that told drivers they were entering Pinecrest—Where Jesus is Lord! it claimed—headlights appeared in the rearview and drew closer fast. I started breathing so fast, trying to catch my breath, that I feared I would hyperventilate at the wheel.

The Village was dark except for the light that shone on the sign and the huge wooden crucifix in front of the college.

Suddenly, the car behind me slowed and its headlights grew smaller in the mirror.

It turned right into an apartment complex called the Mountain Arms, where many of the college's faculty lived.

Tension rushed from my body and I went limp with relief. I drove fast through the Village and started back down the mountain, taking the sharp curves of the steep, narrow road faster than ever before.

Headlights appeared ahead of me in the other lane. For a moment, I considered the possibility that it was a Bollinger, on the look-out for my Volkswagen, ready to take me back to that rambling edifice. But I forced myself to dismiss the notion.

Up ahead, a rush of movement to the left caught my eye. Something was coming down the embankment fast. It stumbled into the middle of the road and stopped. A deer — a buck with a large rack. The tires of the approaching car squealed over the wet pavement, and it went into a skid. It headed for me sideways. The deer bounded forward, in front of me.

The Beetle went off the edge and rolled down toward the stream below. It landed upside-down, wedged between two immense boulders. The oncoming car that had swerved to avoid hitting the deer went over the edge right behind me and landed on top of the Beetle. The man driving, a fifty-four-year-old accountant who worked in the business office at the college, was killed instantly.

I don't remember any of that, though. The last thing I remember is seeing that other car barreling toward me, and the buck springing gracefully through the air. After that, I can recall nothing but a blackness darker than night.

# Nine

When I tried to open my eyes, it seemed they had been glued closed. They were gummy, the lids heavy, and when I finally got them open, the light was too bright and painful, and I closed them again. My throat ached, and my dry mouth tasted like dirty old flannel. I was so weak, I could lift neither of my arms, and when I tried to speak, all that came out was a breathy croak.

The air was cool and smelled of...I could not put my finger on it. The only thing that came to mind was medicine. I heard a distant voice that sounded pinched, tinny, as if it were coming through a speaker: "Dr. Skinner, line two. Dr. Skinner, line two."

I was in the hospital. Either I was wearing a large hat, or my head had been bandaged from just above my eyes on up. I guessed the latter was the case. My entire body ached—my legs, arms, chest, shoulders, back, neck—and my head pounded with a hot, heavy pain. All the pain seemed distant, as if held back for the time being. I could sense, however, that it was growing worse slowly, steadily, closing in on me like a stalker who was growing bold enough to step out of the shadows. I had an intense thirst and wanted some water, but knew I could not sit up. I shifted carefully in bed, trying to find a comfortable position.

Soft footsteps entered the room and a cheerful female voice said, "You're awake!"

I opened my eyes a little, squinted against the painful light. A plump, middle-aged nurse hovered over me.

"How do you feel?" she asked.

I cleared my throat. "Hurt," I said.

"Yes, I'm sure you do. Do you know why you're here? Do you remember what happened?"

"Did I—" I cleared my throat again, licked my lips, closed my eyes. "Drink of water?"

"Sure, sweetie."

I felt the end of a straw touch my lips. Took it in my mouth and sucked hard, gulped the water.

"Slowly, slowly," she said, then pulled it away.

I wanted more, but decided to wait. "Did I…hit that deer?"

"You were in a car accident," she said. "I need to let Dr. Lillianfield know you're awake."

I groped around in my mind for some memory of an accident, but other than the deer and the headlights of another car, I could find nothing. But there was something else there, something urgent.

Then it all came back in a flood of hideous images, remembered smells, and most importantly, the memory of Carla Firth's purse.

I opened my eyes again, blinked a few times. "How long've I been here?"

"Three days."

"Three—are you—" I tried to sit up without fully realizing what I was doing.

"No, no, no," she said, putting a hand on my chest. "Don't try to sit up yet."

"I have to talk to the police. Right away."

"Well …there's an officer right outside your room."

I frowned up at her. "There is? Why?"

She tucked her lower lip between her teeth thoughtfully for a moment, then said,

"You just lie back, okay? I need to call Dr. Lillianfield."

After the nurse left, I closed my eyes and wondered why, after three days, there was a police officer waiting outside my room. Before I could consider any possible reasons, I drifted back to sleep.

When I opened my eyes again, a man in a white coat stood over me.

"I'm Dr. Lillianfield," he said. He had black hair with strands of silver over the ears, wore wire-rimmed glasses, had a silver mustache.

"I need to talk to the police," I said hoarsely.

"Yes, and they want to talk to you," he said with a nod. "But that will have to wait, okay?"

He asked questions—how did I feel, where did I hurt, that sort of thing—and I answered them quietly.

"You're very lucky to be alive, Andy, do you realize that?"

I didn't know how to respond to that, so I didn't.

"You weren't wearing your seatbelt," he said.

"I...wasn't? But I always wear my—" I stopped and closed my eyes, remembering how desperate I had been to get away from the Bollinger house. I had been so afraid, so rushed, I had not put on my seatbelt. "Yeah. I guess I didn't."

"You don't remember anything about the accident?"

I tried again to pull up some memory of what had happened, but nothing would come. I slowly shook my head and said, "No, I don't."

He hesitated, took a deep breath. "I'm afraid I have some bad news for you, Andy."

My mind raced. Had there been someone else in the car with me? I couldn't remember. Was the deer the only thing in the road? Had I run over someone?

"You had to be cut out of your car," he said. "It took a while and it wasn't easy.

You lost a lot of blood, and you have a severe concussion. Both of your legs are broken, the right one in three places. Three of your ribs were broken and your spleen was ruptured. We had to take it out. And, uh...Well, Andy, I'm very sorry, but there's no easy way to say this. Your right arm had to be amputated in order to remove you from the wreckage."

He kept talking, his voice droned on, but I was no longer listening. I lifted my head, ignoring the pain, and looked down at my right arm. Rather, at the place where my right arm should have been. It was gone.

I tried to scream, but all that came out was a whispering squeak.

Dr. Lillianfield was still talking when I passed out.

As I slept, I dreamed of them. The woman with the wet, runny hole in her face...the armless, legless figure that crawled over the floor pulling a toy duck...the guffawing, pregnant, microcephalic woman...and, of course, Matthew Bollinger, with his dangling skin and turkey-wing arm and his incomplete legs in the pants with the cuffs sewn closed. I heard his voice, smelled his house.

I cried out when I woke up and the nurse was at my side again in a few seconds.

"Have a bad dream, honey?" she asked.

"Puh-please, can I have more water?"

I sucked on the straw as if to save my life, and once again, she pulled it away before I was finished.

"You don't want to make yourself sick," she said as she put the cup back on the small table to my left. "The police officer outside is pretty anxious to talk to you. I told him I'd ask if you felt up to it, but if not, I don't want you to worry about it, Andy. He's waited three days, he can wait a little longer."

"He's been waiting outside my room for three days?" I asked. "Why?"

"Well, um..." Her eyes moved from mine and darted around the room. "Why don't you just wait and ask him that, okay?"

"I need to talk to him. Could you send him in, please?"

Seconds later, Perry Milner stood beside my bed in uniform and cap. I knew and liked Perry. Every year, I helped out with the Mount Crag Police Department's Christmas toy drive, and I often had lunch in the diner with him. He took Carrie out on occasion, and the three of us had spent a lot of time talking at the diner's counter.

"I'm really sorry about what happened, Andy," he said hesitantly. "I'm...Well, I'm just...sorry about everything."

"Perry, I've got some things to tell you. Before the accident, I was up at the—"

"Wait, Andy. Before you go on...I've gotta say something."

"What?"

"Well, you've been unconscious the last three days, so I

couldn't...um, since this is the first time I've been able to talk to you—" He took off his cap with one hand and swept the other back over his close-cropped, thinning blond hair. "Andy Sayer... you have the right to remain silent. Anything you say—"

"What?"

"—can and will be used against you in a court of law. You have the right to speak to an attorney—"

"Perry, what the—wait, what're you *doing*?"

"—and to have an attorney present during any questioning. If you cannot afford an attorney, one will be provided for you at government expense. Do you—"

"Perry, what the hell is going on?"

"—understand your rights as I have explained them to you?"

"What're you doing, Perry, why are you—"

"Please answer the question. Do you understand your rights as—"

"Yes, yes, I understand them!" I tried to sit up, but the pain in my head grew unbearable and I dropped back onto the pillow. "Are you *arresting* me?"

He bowed his head a moment, then put his cap back on and nodded once. Quietly, he said, "Andy, you're under arrest for the murder of Carla Firth, Victoria Schmidt, and Anna Quinn."

The last three women to be found dead and mutilated in the woods. My mouth opened, but I couldn't speak. I suddenly felt a bone-deep chill, as if someone had opened a window on an icy winter night.

Perry put his hands on his hips, looked around the room as if searching for something on the walls. When he looked down at me again, he was frowning. "In your car, we found articles of clothing, jewelry, and other personal effects belonging to those three women. There was blood on most of them."

I heard Bollinger's thunderous voice as clearly as if he were in the room: *You don't know it yet, boy, but you gonna hafta come back here 'cause you got nowheres else t'go*!

Determined to sit up in bed, I clenched my teeth and tried to ignore the pain in my head as I attempted to prop myself up on my elbows. But I no longer had two elbows. I could feel my right arm, it moved when I wanted it to move. But it was no longer there.

"I don't think you should be moving around like that, Andy," Perry said. When I started to speak, he added, "And I don't think you should say anything now until you get an attorney. Okay?" He turned and went to the door, looked back at me, and said, "Again, I'm real sorry. About everything."

After he left, I stared at the ceiling—

... *you got nowheres else t'go*!

—and contemplated my situation.

I don't know how much time had passed when the telephone on the table rang. I ignored it at first, just let it ring and ring. But it would not stop. Finally, I reached for it weakly, clumsily, took the receiver from its cradle and put it to my ear. Before I could say hello, a familiar loud voice spoke at the other end of the line.

"Real sorry to hear about your accident, boy," Bollinger said. "That's a *terrible* thing. But I hope it's made y'realize where y'stand. Know what I mean?"

"You son of a bitch," I said. My weak voice failed convey my anger and hatred.

"Oh, now, we can't have *that,* Andy. That kinda talk, thass not very Christian. You need to get y'self right with Jesus, boy, 'cause from what I hear, you in a real spot a trouble. Ever'body's talkin' 'bout it. The story's all over the place."

"Why did you do this?" I asked. "Why did you put that stuff in my car?"

"Well, now, Andy, I'm not sure I know what you're talkin' 'bout." He was silent for several seconds, then: "I told you y'wouldn't have nowheres else t'go, Andy. I meant it."

I said nothing. I wanted to shout at him, scream curses at him, but I was too weak.

"So, boy. You ready to come home where y'belong? You ready to go back t'school so you can take on my bidness for me when the Lord calls me home?"

I laughed quietly, hollowly. He was insane. "I've been arrested. For murder. *Three* murders. I won't be going to school anytime soon."

He returned my laugh with one of his own. "What'm I gonna

hafta do t'get it through your head, boy? I own this mountain an' all the mountains around here. And everything on 'em and around 'em. Don'tchoo unnerstand that? One phone call from me, Andy, and you ain't under arrest no more. One phone call from me to the president a the college, they'd take you in if you was a polka-dotted alien from the planet Jupiter and ate coeds on a stick for lunch. I can fix it so all this's just a stupid mistake, an' ever'body just shrugs their shoulders and goes on with they lives. Or I can fix it so you get the chair. S'up to you, boy."

There was a silence so long that, for a moment, I thought the connection had been severed. Then Bollinger said, "So, whatta y'think, son? You ready t'come home?"

# Ten

Matt put me in the same room where I'd broken the window with the chair. The couch opened into a bed and there was a bathroom attached. Later, when I'm better, he says I can move upstairs.

"You'll be sharin' Dexter's room," he said the day they brought me home. "He's been yackin' about nothin' but you ever since you met, so I promised him you'd be movin' in with him."

Daisy brings me a gift every morning. A bouquet of plastic flowers, an ancient encyclopedia, a box of business-size envelopes, a thimble.

Every evening, Matt comes into my room with three or four of the others—I still haven't met them all—and reads a chapter from the Bible, then leads us in prayer.

Every night, late, Amanda comes in and wakes me. She takes off her robe and lies naked beside me, whispers to me all the things she wants to do when I'm better.

The things she wants to do with me. To me. Smiling, she conjures filthy fantasies about the two of us, and in all of them, we come very close to being caught by Matt, who would be furious, I'm sure. She always excites herself with her own words, and usually masturbates quietly before she leaves. She never uses her hands, but I can hear the soft sounds of wet movement between her legs. Sometimes, she uses her tongue, but when she does that, I close my eyes.

"Daddy says we Bollingers are all exceptional," she whispered one night. "Different. But he says I'm the *most* exceptional, because I'm not like any of the others. I'm different… *inside*."

Children come in and out all day. I read to them from battered old Dr. Seuss books and a collection of Mother Goose tales published in 1924. Making them laugh is the only joy I've had since coming here. Their deformities seem to melt away when they laugh.

But their laughter makes me ache, as well. Because I have already decided what I'm going to do once I get my strength back and I can walk again. I have not yet decided how, though. With so many of them involved, my options are limited. I've narrowed it down to somehow poisoning the food or burning down the house. At first, I wanted only to kill Matt Bollinger. But it did not take long for me to see that he was the glue of the entire family. Without him, they would all be lost. So I will kill them all, even if I kill myself doing it. I think I will be doing them a favor. And if I have to die as well, I just might be doing myself a favor, too.

They are a family that should not be, that never should have been. They are people who never should have been conceived, let alone born. There are days when I hate them all, and days when I feel nothing but pity for them.

I'm not sure which is behind my decision to kill them—my hatred or my pity.

Sometimes it's hard to tell the difference between the two.

# Afterword

First of all, thank you for reading The Folks. There are more books to choose from than ever before, and you chose this one. I am grateful.

Secondly, If you have not yet read the novella, please do not read this Afterword.

It contains spoilers and might compromise your enjoyment of the book. Read *The Folks* first, then come back here.

Some of the harshest criticism my writing has ever received has been leveled at *The Folks*. Fortunately, there wasn't a whole lot of it, but it was out there. The book exploited genetic deformity, they said; it was without compassion and solely for horrific effect, one critic claimed. I'm assuming these critics were new to the horror genre, because creating horrific effect is the whole point. Horror is not only politically incorrect, it is typically incorrect in every way imaginable. It is a genre that routinely defies nature itself, so it will inevitably offend some along the way.

I object, however, to the claim that the book is without compassion. The protagonist is a misfit, an outsider. We are all outsiders in some way and the feeling of not fitting is something familiar to all of us. Our brains are wired to focus on the negative in everything, including ourselves. That trait was no doubt helpful when we lived in the wilderness and had to kill every meal; I'm sure it kept us out of a lot of trouble. These days, however, it can be problematic. When we aim that trait at ourselves, as we inevitably do, it can do a lot of damage over time.

The book's compassion is for human beings, across the

board, whether twisted by their genetics or by the natural negative bias of their own brains.

Great compassion is expressed in the book for the Bollinger infants and children.

After all, they did not ask for their various conditions.

But I'm not sure how much compassion Matthew Bollinger deserves. Remember, he's the guy who did all of this, knowingly and intentionally. He's the head of the family.

Yes, it was done to him first, but he's obviously an intelligent man who knows something of the world and how it works—unlike the family he has kept isolated from the world like some kind of cult—and at some point, he had to have an awareness of what he was doing, the damage he was perpetuating, and he had to make a conscious decision to keep doing it. I'm a little short on compassion for Matthew. As far as I'm concerned, he's the villain here.

Every missing limb and disfigured face, every twisted deformity in that family is an expression of who and what Matthew Bollinger is.

I always advise young writers to never respond to critics. It's simply bad form.

Normally, I do not. And I'm not exactly doing that here.

*The Folks* was published in 2001, a while ago. Since then, people have become much more sensitive. Baseball has been replaced by outrage as the National Pastime.

All that's needed is something at which to aim that outrage. And criticism, unfortunately, has been replaced by bitter personal attacks.

Because it has only been available in a limited edition that's now nearly two decades old, this book will be new to some. And it will be an easy target.

I'm not so much responding to the critics of 2001 as I am anticipating the possible attacks of 2018.

The horror genre has a long history of stories about inbred families. I think it's safe to call it a subgenre by now. The Dead River trilogy by Jack Ketchum—*Off Season* (1980), *Offspring*

(1991), and *The Woman* (2010), which was written simultaneously by Ketchum as a novel and Lucky McKee as a movie—Wes Craven's *The hills Have Eyes* movies, and the incest-packed novels of V.C. Andrews are among the most famous, but many writers have contributed.

I have found some of those stories to be pretty horrifying, but in an enjoyable and entertaining way. Horror is meant to horrify, and I can think of few things more horrifying than being a child in such a family. But these stories usually aren't told from a child's point of view (the novels of V.C. Andrews are an exception). They typically are told from the point of view of an outsider who is then in some way menaced or victimized by the family.

I wanted to tweak the subgenre a little. Most inbred families in horror stories are also cannibals. Not the Bollingers. They are rich and they eat well, but they don't eat people. While they live in an isolated house that climbs the side of a mountain, they are by no stretch of the imagination hillbillies, which is a common trope. Matthew Bollinger is a successful businessman with connections around the world and an unspecified fortune—we just know it's enough for him to be left alone to do as he pleases with his family without anyone knowing about it. And the Bollinger family goes back—*way* back. All the way back to the Mayflower. They've been here from the beginning, and who knows *how* much power and influence Matthew Bollinger really wields. The story is told by an outsider, but not only an outsider to the Bollinger family—an outsider to the world, someone who does not fit because of his disfigurement and who, for that reason, is vulnerable. And rather than being menaced or victimized by the family, Andy is embraced warmly because Matthew wants him to take over the reins in his place.

Instead of writing *The Folks*, with all that hideous deformity, I could have written about a dysfunctional, abusive family with a lot of children, and that abuse could result in a different mental illness in each child, which would bring them nothing but misery and stigmatize them as adults, and I could have blamed each of those mental illnesses on the violent and sexually abusive patriarch of that family.

Well, I maintain that I did *precisely that*—but in my own way.

I don't write the kind of books described above. I read them and enjoy them, but I don't write them. I'm a horror writer, and I write horror fiction. If I wrote the book described above, I think my readers would be annoyed with me.

No matter what genre they write in, I think all writers are essentially writing about the same thing—the human condition. They're writing about that even if they're not writing about humans. Each writer approaches that same subject in a different way, from a different angle, and all of those writers bring their own experience to their work, which is why readers have such a wide variety of genres to choose from when reading fiction.

This particular book falls into the category of horror fiction, which you most likely knew going in. If you found it horrifying and offensive, I have done my job. If you then complain about it and blindly throw accusations at me *because* it horrified and offended you, then you are reading the wrong kind of fiction and you should read something else from now on. Or stop complaining. One or the other.

Fortunately, readers seem to overwhelmingly disagree with those critics. One of the things I'm most commonly asked is when I'm going to write another book in *The Folks* series. It appears to be a favorite among my readers—probably for the very same reasons that it offended those critics in 2001. For those who have enjoyed the first book in the series, I will soon be making *The Folks 2: No Place Like Home* available as an eBook and paperback, and I'm currently at work on the third book in the series, *The Folks 3: Home is Where the Heart is.*

Horror is not for everybody. I cannot think of a single thing that is—and I've tried.

We all like different things for different reasons. That's not a character flaw or an aberration of some kind—it's part of what makes up an individual personality. And without those, we are exceedingly boring. If you've ever spent any time with someone who has no individual personality, you know what I mean.

I'm happy that *The Folks* will now be reaching a wider readership, and I hope those readers enjoy it. But it seems inevitable in this social climate that some will be upset by the book. For them, I want to make the following assurances:

1.) None of the people in this story are real.

2.) Nothing in this story really happened.

3.) No real people with genetic deformities were harmed in the writing of this imaginary story.

If you feel some outrage coming on, keep telling yourself, "It's only a horror story…it's only a horror story…it's only a horror story…"

Keep reading,
Ray Garton
April 15, 2018

# About the Author

Ray Garton has been writing novels, novellas, short stories, and essays for more than 30 years. His work spans the genres of horror, crime, suspense, and even comedy. Live Girls was nominated for the Bram Stoker Award in 1988, and Garton received the Grand Master of Horror Award at the 2006 World Horror Convention. He lives in northern California with his wife Dawn, where he is at work on a new novel.

CROSSROAD
PRESS

www.ingramcontent.com/pod-product-compliance
Lightning Source LLC
LaVergne TN
LVHW050937080826
845145LV00004B/1294

* 9 7 8 1 6 3 7 8 9 9 1 0 6 *

"I'd like to introduce to our congregation today an extraordinary young man, and an exemplary student at Hand of God," Pastor Knotts said in his even, perfectly modulated voice. He sounded like a game show announcer giving a dramatic reading of a newspaper's obituaries. "His name is Andy Sayers and he comes into our loving fold after much hardship and pain."

I wanted to run from the building and never show my face there again. I wanted to strangle Knotts. I wanted to strangle myself. He went on and on and on, and his words melted together into a kind of psychedelic blur of humiliating sound, until he said:

"—of course, that it was God's will." Knotts turned to me with a long-toothed smile, reached out his hand, and I automatically shook it. "I would like to welcome you here to our mountain, Andy, and I want you to know—"

"Wait a second," I said, frowning. "Did...did you just say that this—" I pointed to my face. "—that what happened to my face, did you just say that was... *God's* will?"

His smile faltered as he dropped my hand, stumbled over a few words. "Well, uh, a*hem,* er, we all know the Bible promises that all things work together for—"

"You really believe that God *wanted* this to happen to me?"

The smile was gone and his posture became stiffer than usual—which I, until that moment, had thought to be physically impossible. "As *Christians,* Andrew, we believe that God has a purpose in everything he—"

I raised my voice. "Yes or no, do you believe this was God's will?"

His already creased face wrinkled even more and took on the look of a soft, rotting apple collapsing in on itself. His jaw clenched and he said, "Yes, we *do* believe that it was God's will, Andrew. Of *course* we do."

I spread my arms beseechingly and shouted, "Then why the fuck do you *worship* the sick bastard?"

ISBN 978-1-63789-910-6

For information address Crossroad Press at 141 Brayden Dr., Hertford, NC 27944
A Macabre Ink Production -Macabre Ink is an imprint of Crossroad Press.
www.crossroadpress.com

Crossroad Press Trade Edition

Richard screamed in rage and threw himself at the hag, but he never made it.

A searing wave of heat hit him and flattened him. He lay there on the floor, numb and senseless, choking on his own tears and nausea and helplessness. It was over. He was too late and now there wasn't a damn thing he could do to save Holly.

Not a damn thing.

He tried to rise and the hag snarled at him, rising up like a balloon, stinking and bulging, inflating until it seemed she would burst. A putrescent thing filled with corpse gas and feathered with mold. Slime exuded from her pores and black blood ran from her orifices. The only thing alive about her were those eyes...silver and purple galaxies imploding, crying tears of rank arterial blood.

"Do not interfere, Richard. The time is far past for that. The time of the birthing approaches and you will not obstruct that holy event," she warned him. "If you do, there will consequences. Your wifey can be a corpse bride at my bidding. Her heart will not beat and her lungs will not breathe. She will embrace you as a living hide..."

He began to sob and the hag only cackled.

"When you look upon me again," the beast said, "it will be because I have compelled you to give unto me what is mine by birthright."